Let It Snow, Cowboy

Loved meeting you!

USA TODAY BESTSELLING AUTHOR
JOSEPHINE BLAKE

All Rights Reserved.

No part of this publication may be sold, copied, distributed, reproduced, scraped, or transmitted in any form or by any means, mechanical or digital, including photocopying and recording, or by any information storage and retrieval system without the prior written permission of the author, Josephine Blake, except in the case of brief quotations embodied in critical articles and reviews.

The use of this work for the teaching of generative AI systems is absolutely prohibited.

Publisher's Note: This is a work of fiction. Names, characters, places, and incidents either are the product of the author's imagination or are used fictitiously. Any resemblance to actual persons, living or dead, business establishments, events, or locales is entirely coincidental.

Copyright© 2022 by Josephine Blake. Published by Josephine Blake. *www.awordfromjosephineblake.com*

979-8-3303-5626-3

Cover Design by Covers and Cupcakes LLC. Photography by Bookish Photography. *www.coversandcupcakes.com*

Thank you for purchasing "Let it Snow, Cowboy" by Josephine Blake. Enjoy!

LET IT SNOW, COWBOY

Chapter One

LUCY BENNETT RUBBED HER eyes wearily, shifting her feet on the uneven carpet. A sharp ache was throbbing in the arch of her left foot, and she winced as she settled a fat little Santa Claus onto a velvet-lined pouf by the front door.

It was the day after Thanksgiving, and Lucy had spent the afternoon clearing out the colorful fall displays to make way for the Christmas decorations on the gift shop shelves. Every year, the coming Christmas season seemed to begin earlier than the one before it. Some of the local stores had set out their Christmas décor right after Halloween, but as far as Lucy was concerned, that was far too over-enthusiastic.

The holidays had their time and place, just like everything else.

Lucy reached down to straighten Santa's hat, smiling fondly at his rosy cheeks; then she stood and stretched her arms overhead. Her back gave a little *crack* as she did so. With a grimace, she flipped the sign on the entrance from 'Open' to 'Closed' and flicked off the outside lights.

On her way to the cash register at the back of the store, she pulled the clip from her curly hair, letting it spill down around her shoulders. Her head felt as though it'd been filled with the fluffy white "snow" surrounding the tiny Victorian village in the corner of the store. Lucy wanted nothing more than a hot bath, followed by a book and her cozy, warm bed.

She paused, frowning at a display of snow globes on the shelf situated to the right of the register that she hadn't noticed this morning. They all seemed to feature cozy, winter couples. The one at the fore of the others caught her eye. Inside the watery orb, a woman with curly dark hair—very like her own—was falling into the arms of a handsome man wearing a cowboy hat. Lucy raised her eyebrow. The couple was wearing ice skates.

She hated ice-skating. Ever since she had been a kid and had made an utter fool of herself at a friend's birthday party years ago... Shannon, the owner, must have set out the display the night before. Lucy thought about reorganizing the shelf to shove the ice-skating couple to the back, but she really was extremely tired...

From now until Christmas, her hours would be long and hard. She had been working at the Pansy House gift shop since she was sixteen. Now, at twenty-two, Lucy often wondered mildly if this was all that her life would ever amount to. The thought didn't alarm her in the slightest. She'd been born in the tiny town of Silverton, Oregon, and she'd probably grow old here, content with the quaint placidity that came with small-town life.

Humming tunelessly, Lucy closed out the register, retrieved her coat and purse, and switched off the remaining lights. It was a little after ten. She had stayed a few hours after closing to work on the displays, and her mind balked at the thought of returning in time to open the next morning.

The sound of the door jingling shut behind her was immediately drowned out by the excessive wailing that was echoing from the bar across the street. Sullivan's seemed to be hosting an exuberant open-mic night.

Lucy grimaced as the female singer hit a particularly sour note. It was amazing how when a person drank a bit, they suddenly became a rock star. She loved to sing, but there was no amount of alcohol that could induce her to do *that*! Her best friend, Janie, who worked at the diner across the street, was always attempting to pull Lucy up on stage. But Lucy was stubborn. She would sooner eat yellow snow than participate in an open-mic night in front of the small-town folks she had known her entire life.

She located her old red sedan along the curb and held her key ring up to the streetlight to see. As the correct key slid into the lock, there was a commotion at the entrance of the bar that made Lucy glance up. One of Sullivan's patrons was being shown the door—if being shown the door meant hitting it with your head as you were being thrown out of it.

The man hit the sidewalk hard, his wide-brimmed rancher's hat falling off and skipping to the side. He lay there for a minute, quite still. Lucy peered at him in some concern... he looked vaguely familiar to her somehow...

His body was motionless for several long moments, the flickering neon dancing over his leather-clad shoulders. Then he shifted, and Lucy—realizing she had been staring—quickly unlocked her car door and set her purse down on the passenger seat. She glanced up as she slid behind the wheel, curious, despite herself.

The man on the ground lolled onto his side, his face suddenly illuminated in the streetlights, and on an irritable sigh, Lucy recognized him. *Daniel Moore.*

She'd gone to school a few years behind the boisterous youth Daniel had been in high school, and she recalled nursing a small crush on him. She had been a freshman, and he, a senior. He'd never known Lucy existed.

Cursing herself and bemoaning the task that was about to keep her from her precious bed, Lucy clambered out of her car once more, avoiding a large, slushy puddle. Daniel had sat up by the time she'd reached him, his torso swaying a bit and his head looking heavier than it ought to.

"You good there, bud?"

The sloppy version of her high school crush raked his hand through his tousled dark hair, looking up at her with bloodshot eyes. "Lanky Lucy?"

Lucy blushed crimson. He *did* remember her, though it wasn't in a particularly pleasant manner—why would it be? Back then, she'd been skinny beyond belief *and* flatter than a pancake on all sides. She snorted. At least one thing had changed for the better.

Frowning, she held out her hand. "Here. Let me help you." She almost toppled over as he struggled to stand up, all his weight on her slender fingers.

"You had a crush on me in high school," he teased, grinning stupidly. "My buddies ribbed me about it all senior year."

He wrapped an arm around her shoulders as she tried to balance him and waved a finger at her accusingly, as though she'd deceived him somehow. "You were just a gangly teenager with braces, straight as a board. Boys had more curves than you did back then."

"Shut up," she said through her teeth, as she struggled to remain upright under his weight. "You need to get a bite to eat and some coffee." She glanced around, noting with dismay that the diner two blocks down had closed at its usual ten o'clock.

Daniel was eyeing her, still grinning like an idiot. "You've filled out in all the right places." His hand dropped from her shoulder to her waist, and he lost his balance as she threw him from her.

"I prefer my men sober, thanks," she bit out. "What an interesting man you've grown into, Mister Moore."

He chuckled at her, swaying slightly. "So, you-a think I'm cute?"

Her frown deepened. "That's not what I said."

He raised his hand in the air as he attempted to stumble away down the sidewalk. "Too late! You like me! You *love* me!" He kept repeating it until he tripped on his own feet and dropped back to the sidewalk, giggling madly.

Lucy sighed. She should just get back in her car and go home. This moron wasn't worth the headache, and she had to work tomorrow. She glared at the drunken man now snoring quite contentedly on the concrete, then shivered. It was cold and getting colder. *He'll freeze to death, and it'll be your fault.*

It'll be his own dang fault, the most annoyed part of her brain argued back.

Rolling her eyes so far back in her head that it hurt, Lucy approached and prodded Daniel with her foot. "Hey. Idiot. You alive?"

No response.

With a growl of frustration, she ran to get her car. It felt like the temperature had dropped ten degrees in the last ten minutes. She couldn't just leave him out here, idiot or no. She wouldn't be able to sleep tonight.

She pulled her car around to where she had left Daniel and sat for a moment with the engine idling, trying to think what to do. He was at least moving again. He had pushed himself upright and kept patting the top of his head.

She opened the passenger side door and went to help him up.

The gaze he turned on her was glassy and bewildered. "Where's my hat?"

Lucy groaned. Cowboys and their hats! "We'll get it in a minute," she told him. "First, we need to get you in the car." She tugged on his shoulders. "You're gonna have to help me, big guy. I can't carry you on my own."

He did his best to stand up. Once upright, he leaned against the hood of her car, squinting around.

Lucy tapped his shoulder. "You gonna make it?"

"If this dog-nardit sidewalk would just..." He made a shushing motion with his hand and giggled feebly. She shook her head.

She placed one of his arms around her shoulders and took hold of his waist, groaning inwardly as his considerable weight sagged onto her yet again. "Just a few steps. Can you do that?"

She poured him into the passenger seat a handful of shaky moments later, securing his seatbelt, and swiping at her brow. He was still patting his head.

His hat. She ought to leave it. More than a little annoyed, Lucy jogged across the icy sidewalk to where Daniel's cowboy hat had settled into a puddle of slush and retrieved it with a grumble.

As she slid into the driver's seat, she glanced over at her unwelcome companion. His dark hair flopped into his eyes with an annoyingly careless, tousled handsomeness, and the scruff on his cheeks brushed against the collar of his coat—prickly, and unshaven. He still had the sharp jawline and small cleft in his lip that had caught her attention in high school, but he had a tattoo now. She frowned at the sight of the ink lines she could just see skating up over his collar along the side of this neck. It was impossible to tell what it was in this light, but Lucy could not help but feel... slightly disappointed. She had never really been a fan of inked guys—or drunk ones, for that matter.

Daniel Moore let out a tremendous, grunting snore that made Lucy flinch with the volume. If not for the seatbelt, he would have slid straight down to the floorboard. She shook her head again, turned the wheel, and guided her studded tires carefully onto Main Street. The tidy little avenue was shining with the recent rain and snow that had dappled it on and off throughout the day.

Daniel's head was resting against the cold window, his breath fogging the glass. He was going to feel something awful in the morning.

Unsure where to head at first, she took a left and then reached over to prod Daniel hard in the chest. "Hey, where do you live?"

"Eh?!" Daniel startled awake.

"I said, where do you live??"

"Over that way," he mumbled.

"Over—" but he was snoring once more.

Lucy sighed, then realized her only course of action was to lug this moron home with her and let him sleep it off. "Lord, give me patience," she whispered, swiping at her tired eyes. She glanced at him again. Then forced her eyes back to the road. It didn't *really* matter—because she would never be interested in a drunken cowboy who spent his Friday nights doing karaoke with impossibly bad singers—but he was still kinda... maybe... a little cute.

She pulled up in front of the tiny house that she rented on the corner of Russel and Eighth. It wasn't much, but it was difficult to afford anything more on a retail clerk's wages. The little place got her out of her mother's house and on her own, so it was certainly worth it. At least here, she could be herself.

There was a tidy little front garden covered in decaying leaves and a naked maple tree, its branches bending a bit in the breeze. Two houses down, the Cassett family had evidently spent the day decorating. Their house was the only one on the street already twinkling with Christmas lights. The overall feeling of her neighborhood was... homey—if not quite *home.*

She focused on Daniel thoughtfully. With the temperature dropping, she could hardly just abandon him in the car. However, that meant somehow maneuvering him up the little set of stairs and into the house, and she was afraid he was too far gone this time to rouse.

Lucy unbuckled her seatbelt and circled around the drive to the other side of the car, slipping a bit on a patch of ice as she opened the passenger door. Laying a firm hand on his shoulder, she gave Daniel a hearty shake, but he only groaned.

"C'mon, you big lug. Wake up." She pinched him, hard, but received a similar response. Staring around in dismay, a thought struck her, and she reached for a chunk of the icy puddle she had just slipped in, grinning impishly.

His eyes shot open as the ice slipped into the neck of his red flannel. "What in the whole heck?!!" Within moments he was jittering about in the passenger seat like a rabid racoon. "Cold. Cold. Cold. Cold," he hissed through his teeth, his eyes only half open as he struggled.

"Good," chuckled Lucy, trying not to laugh. "Now just... if you could move your foot, and... No! No! No! No! No!" Lucy finished on a groan. Having divested himself of the ice, the impudent man's head had slipped back against the headrest once more. She jabbed him hard, and his eyes flickered. "Listen. Stupid. Hey, LIS-

TEN." Lucy grabbed his chin. "Get your ungrateful rear end out of my car before I..." As she released his seat belt, he toppled sideways, only just catching himself on the car door.

"Okay." Lucy was sweating now, but she reached down for Daniel's armpits and heaved him upright.

He mumbled something unintelligible as he made a very poor attempt to support himself, and finally, the two began making shaky progress up the short drive to the front door.

She talked him up the three steps, then leaned against the doorjamb for support while she fumbled with her keys. Of all the stupid, ridiculous situations to have gotten herself into.... She was muttering foully beneath her breath... "I imagine your mother would tan your hide, Daniel Moore... I ought to tan your hide! *Someone* ought to, at least..."

The sofa was right next to the door, and when it swung open, Lucy nearly cried with relief and promptly tipped the massive cowboy sideways. He tilted, cried out, and then sprawled atop the cushions, bleary-eyed and bewildered. Lucy tore off her coat and scarf without sparing him a second glance, still muttering.

Around the corner, in the kitchen, she filled a glass with frigid water from the purifier in the refrigerator and downed two before filling it for a third time and carrying it into Daniel.

He was still looking around blearily. "S'not my couch," he said, swiveling his head from side to side. "S'not my place. S'not Dad's place. Where... Water!" He nearly knocked the glass from Lucy's hand in his drunken enthusiasm.

"Would you mind... terribly... getting those off my couch?" She indicated the muddy boots that were now leaving smears over the chocolate-colored leather.

"S'your place?"

"Yes," Lucy responded stoically.

"S'nice."

"You're dumping water on my floor."

"Sorry. I think I 'ad a bit—" He raised his fingers to display them a miniscule distance from one another. "—too much at Sully's."

"Gee, you think?"

"Should... Mmmm... Probably not stay at yours. People will talk."

"What do you think this is? The 1850's?"

At that moment, a slow *tap-tapping* of paws on hardwood announced the lazy arrival of her old rescue pup, Shiloh. The Australian Shepherd fixed his icy blue gaze on Daniel for a moment as he entered the living room and then looked up at Lucy doubtfully, as if to say, "Is that a human?"

"Woof," mumbled Daniel feebly, and he giggled. Then, without warning, he slipped sideways against the cushions and began to snore once more. Lucy only just caught hold of his water glass before it dropped to the floor.

"Moron," she grumbled, and she stomped back to the kitchen.

She returned a moment later, glared at the boots Daniel hadn't managed to remove, and set about attempting to tug them from his feet. By the time she had managed it, she was sweating again, but she allowed herself a grudging smile when she saw his socks. They were covered with dogs and cats, all wearing little cowboy hats.

After wrestling the man into a supine position... "Should just push you onto the floor." She went to the closet and took out a down comforter. "Going to have to wash this... maybe twice."

Her unwanted companion of the evening finally situated, Lucy took her grumbling to the bedroom, patting her leg for her grumpy, retired farm dog. Shiloh came, limping a bit with winter stiffness, but paused at the bedroom door to turn back and give a little, soft warning bark to the stranger on the couch, just so he knew Shiloh was prepared to defend Lucy if necessary.

The bedroom door shut and—for good measure—locked behind her, Lucy wearily removed her clothes and changed into her favorite sweatshirt and leggings. She washed her face and brushed her teeth in the adjoining bathroom, grabbed her book, and settled into bed. Shiloh was already curled up at the foot of the bed, his eyes fixed on the black gap beneath the door.

Lucy rubbed her dog's ears. "He's harmless," she muttered reassuringly. "Perfectly harmless."

⋅•♥•♥•♥•⋅

Daniel rolled over, burying his face in the pillow, trying to silence the air. His head was throbbing so mercilessly that he thought he could actually feel the individual veins in his temples pulsing. His throat was raw, as though he'd attempted to gargle bits of gravel, and his joints were all aching as though they'd all been yanked in several different directions the night before.

A strange, unfamiliar exhale and damp moisture against the back of his neck made his mind seize with a sudden panic. What had he done last night? Where was he?? His mind was dancing around, playing images from the night before on fast-forward. The sound of truly atrocious singing. Shouting. The smell of wet concrete when he'd been tossed out of Sullivan's on his ear. Freezing air on his head... Drat it all. Had he lost his hat? There had been a girl, of that he was fairly certain. A girl he'd known from school... Sick with dread, Daniel tensed and rolled, nearly ending up on the floor.

Finding himself abruptly face-to-face with two blue eyes and a furry muzzle, Daniel's eyes shot wide open, and a wave of enormous relief flooded through his sore brain. Seeing he was awake, the dog gave him a sloppy, wet welcome.

Daniel sputtered and sat up to fend off the dog's advances. Rubbing his itching eyes with one hand, he reached out to scratch the excitable animal behind its ears with the other. "Well, hey," he croaked. "Who are you?"

"His name is Shiloh."

Daniel's head jerked up. A petite gal with a sharp, inquisitive sort of face, and curly hair the color of an amber ale was standing in the hall across from him. She was wearing an overlong, creamy-colored sort of sweater, tight jeans, and warm, fuzzy boots. She looked cozy, in a classy sort of way, like she could either curl up on the couch and snuggle in for a good movie or head off to organize an entire office space. He recognized her at once as a girl he'd gone through his last year of high school with. She had been cheery, but shy, and her name was… Lacy. No.

"Lucy?"

Her hair was piled into a loose bun at the top of her head, and her expression was irritable. It darkened further when he spoke, and Daniel feared he'd got the name wrong for a moment before she said:

"I believe you called me 'Lanky Lucy' last night."

He grimaced. "That was mean."

"It was a bit, yes."

"You don't look anything like you did in high school."

"Oh, thanks," she said sarcastically, rolling her eyes heavenward.

Daniel pinched the bridge of his nose. His head was going to explode. "That's not what I… I meant that you look good."

"You'll forgive me if I'm not utterly flattered to be complimented by the drunken idiot that spent an impromptu night on my couch."

"Understandable," he mumbled. "Could I use the bathroom?"

She pointed, and the room blurred a bit as Daniel gained shaky feet. Her dog, Shiloh, skittered back to make room for him to pass, his tail wagging hopefully.

"How do you like your eggs?" she asked, marching past him through a framed archway that he guessed led to the kitchen.

"You don't need to—"

"What?!" she yelled as loudly as she could from a foot away, grinning. Her eyes were dancing with mischief. If he'd had the energy to bend down and grab one, he would have thrown a pillow at her.

"Suppose I deserved that," he muttered, his hands at his ears.

"You have no idea!" She clapped her hands loudly, smiling all the while. "Get a move on! I've got to go to work! Chop! Chop!"

He winced with each impact of her hands and turned about to locate the bathroom.

"Door on the right. I'm making a scramble," she declared.

He poked his head back around the corner. "You don't need to bother with that. I've already been enough trouble."

"You can say that again." She gave him an offhand look. "I'm having breakfast anyway. It's just as easy to make two servings as one."

He nodded his thanks, swallowed roughly, and then glanced down at himself. "I hate to ask this, but would it be okay if I took a quick shower?"

Lucy grinned at him. "Good call. You're a bit ripe."

Daniel chuckled. A few minutes later, ensconced in a frilly, beach-themed bathroom, he ran the cold out of the pipes and stepped into a hot shower with a sigh of relief. The heat massaged a bit of the pain away, and tension began to release as he searched for soap. Finding only a fruity gel that seemed to have tiny blue rocks in it, he shrugged, scrubbed up, and emerged feeling at least ten percent more human than when he'd gone in... and vaguely relieved. Judging by this perfectly ordered bathroom and the singular, pink razor he had spotted on the shelf in the shower... there was no male presence anywhere in this house. That meant that Lucy might just be single.

He smelled the delicious scent of bacon wafting in the air through the steam, and his stomach rumbled in response as he followed his nose.

Lucy was standing in a brilliantly yellow kitchen, sliding eggs onto a plate atop a white countertop. "You look like you feel better. Coffee's there," she indicated the pot with a nod of her head.

"Thank you." He looked around as he filled his mug. White cabinets, white countertops, stainless appliances, and a wooden sign on the wall that read, *Do What Makes Your Heart Happy.* Everything else in the kitchen was yellow. The hand towels were dotted with yellow flowers. The yellow patterned container of utensils on the countertop had a label that read, *a spoonful of sugar.* Even the paper towel holder was yellow.

"You like yellow," he observed, as he scooped up a serving of eggs and placed them on his yellow polka-dotted plate, along with two slices of bacon and a toasted piece of *Dave's Killer Bread.* "This looks good. I haven't had a hot breakfast since..." His voice drifted off. The pain of that hurt more than his head.

Lucy didn't say anything. The look on her face told him she understood. In a town this small, she likely knew his entire life story.

He looked at her, *really* looked at her. She was eye-catching, but not in the conventional way. There was just something about her that made her stand out. Her hair was an undyed shade of dark amber blonde. Her face bore minimal makeup. It was her eyes, though, that really got him. When she looked at him with those leaf-green, elvish sort of eyes, it felt as if she was not just looking at him, but *inside* him. To say it was unnerving was mild. What was she seeing? *A sloppy drunk. That's what,* he answered himself. He shook away the thought and glanced around the cozy house, raising his coffee to his lips. "I like this."

She shrugged her shoulders, and her sweater pulled up and down against her jeans. "It's not much, but at least I have my own space."

He looked at her. "Wasn't your mother a Miss Silverton?"

Her hand tightened on her fork. He had hit a nerve. "She was."

Shiloh, sensing his mistress was unhappy, moved to her side and bent his head against her leg. Lucy rubbed his ears absentmindedly.

"I need to be at work in thirty minutes. I assume your car is close to Sullivan's?"

He nodded. "Thanks for not letting me drive."

She laughed. "The thought never even crossed my mind. You were so out of it; I wouldn't have been able to live with myself."

Daniel took another bite of eggs. "I don't usually do that, you know?"

Lucy raised her eyebrows skeptically. "That's not the rumor that went around in high school."

He leaned against the counter, pretending to be examining a cookbook that lay open there as he reached for another piece of toast. "That was a while back. I like to think I've matured a bit since then."

Lucy almost spit out her coffee as she let out a snort. "You could have fooled me!" She took a sip from a glittery yellow water bottle that sat beside her.

"Seriously," he said as he took another sip of coffee. "Last night was... unusual for me. I never drink that much. I just felt... a bit out of control."

She gave him a speculative look. "Do tell."

Suddenly, Daniel felt strangely exposed. His instinct was to close up and shut down. If he didn't think about it, it didn't exist.

She kept you out of jail, buddy, an annoying voice whispered in the back of his mind. So, Daniel took a breath that seemed to fill him with the scent of strawberries and kept it vague. "My father and I aren't... getting along right now. He wants me to be exactly like him. Make the same choices he made in life."

Lucy gave a bitter laugh. "Boy, do I know how that feels."

"Do tell," he said with a half-smile, throwing her words back at her and changing the subject in one fluid move.

She stared pensively into her mug. "It's nothing—nothing that I feel like talking about with a stranger, at least."

The rejection stung. "Sorry. I didn't mean to pry."

"Yes, you did," she said, as she took her plate and scraped its remnants into Shiloh's yellow dog bowl beside a large silver trash bin. "But so did I. So, the fact is, I will never be my mother. She's perfect. I'm not. End of story."

"Sounds familiar. But... what exactly do you—"

She lowered her eyes. "I don't look much like my mother... it bothers her that I'm not..." She sighed and rolled her eyes to the ceiling. "That I'm not..."

Suddenly he got it, and when he did, he was angry with himself for missing it. "She's your typical kind of... well... Barbie-doll pretty, right?" he said, trying very hard not to further insult his host, and bring to mind the photo that hung in the local diner. It was a picture of Lucy's mother, blonde and fabulous, standing on top of a float in the local parade. "You have a different look. Pretty," he clarified quickly. "But you don't look much like her."

Lucy laughed derisively. "I've heard that before. My mother never cared for it much when people said it. She says that I look like my father."

"Where is your father?" Daniel asked.

She looked off to the side, rubbing Shiloh's neck. "He left when I was ten."

He started to say something, but Lucy, having glanced at the ornate clock on the wall, jumped up in a panic. "We have to go! I'm going to be late!" She rushed him out of the house and practically pushed him into the car.

As they drove back into the main part of town, Daniel felt a wave of guilt rush over him for calling her "Lanky Lucy" the night before. His drunken, idiotic self had been unintentionally cruel—and Daniel did not like to think of himself as a cruel person. What was more, she had taken him in despite it, thoroughly protecting him from himself.

"For what it's worth, I owe you one heck of an apology," he said, trying to gauge her expression. "For what I said… and for acting the drunken fool."

When Lucy shook her head and smiled a sad little smile in response, his heart ached. A piece of that whiskey-colored hair slid over her cheek, and his eyes followed it. "What did you say that wasn't true?" she said, masking her discomfort with another laugh.

Without really thinking, or experiencing any awkwardness, Daniel slid his hand over the steering wheel, covering hers for half a moment. "I didn't know you then."

She gave him a darting glance. "And now?"

He squeezed her hand. "I *want* to know you. I told you," He removed his hand and tweaked a button on his coat with a little chuckle. "Matured."

"Yeah, no, I still don't see it." She pulled up in front of the gift shop. "Are you parked close by?"

Daniel pointed to an old red Chevy truck a few spaces down from Sullivan's. "That's mine."

She got out of the car, and Daniel paused, thinking hard before he followed suit.

She was collecting her purse from the back of the car as she said, "Take care, Daniel. Try not to pull a stunt like that again. You might not be lucky enough to end up in *my* car next time."

He shut his door with a metallic *thud*, took a breath, then marched around to her side of the car. Leaning against the trunk, he faced a Lucy who was clearly in a hurry to clock in. He grinned. "Let me take you to dinner tonight."

"Daniel, I've got to—" but then she appeared to register what he'd said, she paused, then said, "that's probably not a great idea."

"Oh, *contraire*, I think it's a very *great idea* indeed."

She made to sidle past him, but he took a step to the left and blocked her path, grinning coyly.

"I'll think about it. But I have to work the entire day. We don't even close until seven..."

She took a deliberate step forward. He moved back. She took another step.

"I really have to clock in!" she cried exasperatedly.

He kept pace with her until they were only three feet from the front door of the Pansy House Gift Shop, but when she tried to step forward again, instead of stepping back, he froze, and she bumped right into his chest.

She leapt back, an increasingly familiar expression of annoyance on her face.

"Daniel... uugh! Yes, fine." He could tell she was agreeing out of sheer desperation to clock in on time, but a rush of victory spread through his chest, and he winked.

"Perfect. I'll see you at seven." Then, on an instinct, he swiped that little strand of hair back from her cheek, and she blushed very prettily. "Looking forward to it."

JOSEPHINE BLAKE

Chapter Two

Lucy rang up the last customer's purchase and went to lock the door while she took the drawer back and counted the cash. She was a little disappointed, though not surprised, that Daniel had not shown up at seven. She had been peeking through the various shelves toward the windows as they darkened, half-expecting his smirking face to appear at any moment.

While he had been absolutely, completely obnoxious the night before, Daniel had been downright adorable this morning in an embarrassed, repentant sort of way. She hadn't expected that. Heck, she hadn't even expected him to still be there when she got up in the morning. But... he had been... and their casual morning banter—apart from the obvious topics neither of them had wanted to discuss—had been weirdly comfortable. She thought on this as she slipped a rubber band around the like bills, stacked them, and headed for the safe.

Lucy then clocked out and flicked out the overhead lights. Pausing to pull the chain on a frilly little lamp shaped like a teapot, she shrugged into her coat and braced herself for the cold. As she approached the front of the store, however, she noticed a figure had materialized just to the right of the front door. His back was to her, so she couldn't see his face—but a little bubble of hope inflated in her stomach.

She approached cautiously. She'd learned over the years to be wary of strangers when she was closing up the store. Once upon a time, she'd had a stalker who would call the store just before closing and mutter uncomfortable things to her, down to describing the clothes she was wearing. The police had patrolled the entire block for over a month until the calls stopped.

The posture of the man outside was stiff, his shoulders high, fending off the cold. He was jostling back and forth on the spot, his hands deep in his pockets. Lucy relaxed when she spotted the edge of a tattoo on the side of his neck.

She tugged open the front door, and without looking up from the keys in her hand she said, "Feeling better?"

He turned, giving her a sheepish look that—curse him—only endeared him to her further. "The only thing hurting now is my pride." He shuffled across the sidewalk and opened the door to the passenger side of his truck. "Dinner? I was thinking maybe Copper

Town? I'm assuming you've been. Do you like it?"

Lucy nodded appreciatively. "It's one of my favorites."

He took her hand, helping her clamber up into the old pickup. Lucy noticed his hand was rough with calluses, a casualty born from working on a cattle ranch his entire life. He shut the door, winked, and made his way around the truck to the other side, practically skipping.

"You're in a good mood," she remarked, grinning.

"And why shouldn't I be? I'm about to have dinner with a lovely young woman."

He placed his arm along the back of her seat as he edged out of the curbside parking space. Lucy caught the faintest scent of soap with spicy, oaky undertones, and found herself taking long, deep breaths for a moment.

"Are you okay?" he asked.

She felt a blush stain her cheeks as she realized she'd gone quiet. "It's nothing. It's just been a long day, and I'm glad to be able to sit back for a minute, finally."

"And you started it off with me." He grimaced. "I'm sure that didn't help."

"You were quite the unanticipated curveball," she agreed, stretching her arms forward until her fingertips touched the dashboard. She gave him a wicked look. "By the way, I really liked your socks."

His eyebrow raised, and his eyes darted from the road to her face in momentary confusion. "Huh?" Then it appeared to click into place. "So, I like cats and dogs. I live on a ranch. I'm thinking of getting a pair with raccoons on them."

Lucy chuckled in response. "I have a racoon that comes to my back door stoop every night, begging. He's a big fan of pecan swirls."

"Why does that not surprise me?"

They settled into an easy silence as they drove to the restaurant.

Copper Town, one of the newer restaurants in Silverton, wasn't too crowded, and they were seated quickly. Lucy took off her coat, laying it on the chair next to her, and quirked a mischievous eyebrow in Daniel's direction. "I'm warning you—after last night, I am definitely ordering dessert."

A red flush crept up the edge of his tattoo, and he rubbed it, seeming not to realize. "I haven't had a night like that in... a really long time. I feel like a fool. There was no reason you should have helped me, either. Especially after I was so rude..."

"Really. If it's so unusual for you, something must have happened to make you—" She sighed and trailed off, tapping the corner of her menu. "You mentioned your father this morning." Her tone was completely non-judgmental. It behooved her to discover what had driven this man to such a degree of imbecilic behavior... because she really did want to believe that it was a one-off sort of thing.

A blond waiter arrived with a cheerful, "Hey, folks! What can I get for you tonight?" And Lucy realized she hadn't even glanced at the menu yet.

"Cheddar Bacon Burger for me," said Daniel, "And we'll start with those little... toast things."

"Crostini? We've got avocado guac, hummus, or cheese fondue for those."

"Cheese fondue, please." Daniel smiled to make sure Lucy agreed, and then the waiter turned to her.

"Blackened Mahi Tacos, please," she said off the top of her head, remembering having had them before and liked them.

"Excellent, back in a flash! Looks like your drinks are at the bar." The waiter vanished into the bar portion of the restaurant, and there was an abrupt silence between them. Above the gentle chatter of the other patrons, Shania Twain sang about how her heart had changed her mind. *Gol' darn gone and done it...*

Lucy was almost afraid Daniel would take the opportunity to change the subject. He didn't.

He took a sip of his water, and the ice cubes clinked against his glass as he replaced it on the table between them. "My father and I had an argument," he said on a long exhale. "Another one... a big one. He really got to me this time, and I think we both said a lot of things that are going to be hard to forget." His expression became pensive. "I'm just... not him. He doesn't seem to understand that."

The waiter brought their drinks. Lucy had ordered a deep red cabernet—an awful choice to pair with her fish tacos, really, but she hadn't thought of that when she ordered. Daniel stuck to tea, which she thought was a wise choice, considering.

Daniel stared at his glass's contents. "He wants me to stay on the ranch. He wants to groom me to run it one day."

"And I take it you don't have any interest in doing so," Lucy stated rather than asked, swirling her wine around in her glass and inhaling deeply.

Daniel watched her with his head cocked to the side, then he shook his head.

"I've only seen people drink wine like that in movies," he commented grinning. Then he went on, "Don't get me wrong. I love working the ranch, but it's not my sole focus. I've been doing this my whole life. I know it like the back of my hand. For some people, that would be enough, but I want something that challenges me, something that is just a bit… different."

She took a sip of her wine, savoring the notes of spice and blackcurrant. "So, what is it you want to do?"

"Promise not to tell?" he asked with the solemnness of a child.

"Scout's honor," she said, making the sign with her hand.

Daniel appeared skeptical. "You were never in the Scouts."

She shrugged her shoulders. "Technicalities, but a promise is a promise. Do you want me to pinky promise? Will that work?"

He grinned, holding up his hand. "Pinky promise?"

She hooked her little finger around his. "Pinky promise."

The waiter brought out their appetizer. Lucy thanked him and took a crostino from the plate, crunching into it. She looked at Daniel pointedly. "I pinky promised. You're honor-bound now."

He placed a crostino on his own plate and sat back in his chair. "I want to do something more... creative. My brain *needs* it. I took up photography in high school. I've even taken some formal classes... sold some stuff here and there... But my dad calls it a hobby. He refuses to think I could do anything real with it at all.

"I *know* I could make a real go of it, but all of my time goes to the ranch. I don't have enough time... and Dad won't allow me enough time..."

"Doesn't he have any other hired hands who can step up?" she asked sympathetically.

Daniel shook his head. "I've tried that angle. He won't bite."

Taking another crostino from the plate, Lucy drowned it in cheese while she said, "I mean, does he really have a choice? Nobody is really making you stay."

"He's my father. I won't do that to him, not after everything that he's... that *we've* been through."

She lowered her eyes. What Daniel said made sense. His mother had died a little over three years ago in a car accident. His father had been the one driving. A soul can only take so much. "What are you going to do?"

"I don't know," he said, sighing. "I'm stuck between a rock and a hard place with it. Do I choose what he wants and wake up thirty years from now regretting the life I made, or do I follow my instincts... and then hurting my dad becomes my greatest regret? It's an either-or situation. There is no compromise with my father. He made that very clear yesterday."

"I'm so sorry. I can't imagine trying to make a choice like that."

What he said struck a familiar chord. She swirled her glass again in thought, then inhaled as she took a sip.

"In a way, we seem to have a bit in common—at least where our folks are concerned," she told him. "After my father left, I felt responsible for my mother's happiness, but I've always fallen short. My mother would never say it, but I think she sees me as an uncomfortable reminder of my father. I mean, I know she loves me, but I think it gets to her sometimes..." Lucy reached across the table, covering his hand with hers. "I just... I just know the last few years have been tough on you, that's all. I get it, and I'm so sorry."

His fingers curled into hers. In the silence of that moment, they spoke volumes.

The waiter coughed subtly, discreetly alerting them to his presence. Upon acknowledgment, he placed their plates on the table and slipped away with a smile once they assured him their needs were completely met.

"I would love to see your work sometime," Lucy said, as she lifted her first taco. "I have a lot of admiration for anyone who can truly capture the beauty or heartbreak of a moment. 'A picture is worth a thousand words,' and all that. No statement has ever been more true."

Daniel looked at her uncertainly, munching on his burger. "Do you mean it?"

"Would I have asked if I didn't?"

"I suppose not," he said. "It just feels sort of weird to finally talk about it. Even my best friends don't really know. I've never really said it aloud to anyone but Dad. I guess I always felt like... like I couldn't be both. Cowboy photographer? That's not a thing." He chuckled, and then gave her a searching look. "You're easy to talk to."

Lucy grinned back, meeting his eyes—more boldly than she had looked at anyone in a long time. "So are you." *Those eyes. They're still the bluest eyes I've ever seen.* She might be melting a bit... Mentally shaking herself, Lucy looked away, pretending to be interested in her food.

"When do you have a day off?" he asked, pushing his fingerling potatoes around with his fork. "Maybe I can show you then?"

"Tomorrow's a Sunday, so the store is closed," Lucy said in a rush, and then too late, hoped she didn't sound over eager. She suddenly felt like she was a freshman in high school all over again.

"Should I come get you, say around one tomorrow?" he asked.

"I can head over to your place around then," Lucy told him, shaking her head. "No reason to come get me."

"Nah. I wasn't much of a gentleman last night," he argued. "Let me be a gentleman tomorrow. I do have a bit of cowboy charm around here somewhere..." He glanced mockingly from side to side, then down at his pockets, and she noticed his pointed boots and grinned. They were the same ones she had tugged off his feet the night before, no longer muddy, but polished to a glow. He had cleaned up good... and he had done it to impress her.

There was definitely something to be said about cowboy charm.

・▼・▼・♥・▼・▼・

The next day, Daniel pulled up to Lucy's quaint little house at one o'clock on the nose. He heard Shiloh let out a grumpy *bark* when he knocked, and he waited patiently on the stoop, trying and failing to look masculine and impressive in the glaring afternoon sunshine.

Lucy answered the door. She was dressed in jeans, a striped t-shirt, and brown boots, and she was tugging on a tan overcoat as she nudged Shiloh away from the porch. Her dark blonde hair was loose around her face. Her eyes stood out like emerald gems. Her casual beauty was alarming. Daniel blinked as she stood aside, inviting him in. "Right on time. I'm impressed!"

He crooked his head sideways at her in question. "Were you expecting less?"

She chuckled. "Okay. Let me introduce you to my timing rules. Don't say you will be here at 2:00 and arrive at 1:45 or earlier. Don't say you will be here at 2:00 and arrive at 2:30 or later. I give a little more room on the late side. Anything outside of those boundaries requires a phone call. I hate early birds. Twenty minutes ago, I was drying my hair. You didn't need to see me before that!"

Daniel chuckled. "I've never known anyone that had it so well thought out."

She gave him a sheepish grin and shrugged as if to say, *I am who I am.* "I just provided you the highlights from the first chapter of my instruction manual. You're welcome."

"I appreciate it. Might need to read the rest of the book." He winked. "Ready, then?"

The responding look on her face made his heart soar with a fearful amount of hope. She reached for a scarf hanging on a hook near the door and then said, "I just need to let Shiloh out for a minute."

"We can take him with us," Daniel said as he bent to rub the dog beneath his chin. "I bet he would like to run around on the ranch. Wouldn't you, boy? He looks... Australian Shepherd? They're herding animals." Daniel's hand paused its massage as he spoke to Lucy, which was *not* to Shiloh's liking. He tapped him lightly with his paw to make Daniel aware that he was falling down on the job.

Lucy let out a little laugh as Daniel crouched down and really scrubbed Shiloh behind the ears. "That's his signature move. That's how he hooked me."

Daniel looked up at her quizzically. "What do you mean?"

Lucy leaned down next to Shiloh, running her hand along his fur. "I was at the Humane Society looking for a grown dog. I wanted the companionship. I was dead set against getting a puppy. I walked by his kennel, and he tapped on the window. One look into those baby blue eyes, and I was a goner."

He chuckled. "Smart boy. He knew a good thing when he saw it." Shiloh flipped clear over on his back to display his belly. "If I thought it would work for me, I'd tap on a window if you walked by. Maybe you would take me in, too."

Lucy stood up. "I did take you in. Remember? And there was no tapping, just downright obnoxious self-endangerment."

Daniel straightened as well, a mischievous glint in his eyes. "But you didn't keep me."

Rolling her eyes to the ceiling, she shook her head at his cheeseball-ness, grinning. "You're cute, but Shiloh's cuter." She grabbed a leash from the table and attached it to her dog's blue collar. "Let's get going before I change my mind."

Daniel held the door of the truck open for Lucy as she and Shiloh made their noisy, clattering way into the vehicle. Shiloh made sure to position himself between them, instinctively acting as their chaperone. Daniel had to give him credit. He might have been tempted to hold Lucy's hand if the dog had sat against the window. Instead, reaching around to lay his arm over the back of the seat to reverse his truck down the driveway, his fingers brushed against the back of Lucy's neck. Her hair tickled at his fingertips, softer than silk. He glanced up to see her looking at him over Shiloh's back.

He left his hand there.

When they pulled up to a log cabin-style home built beneath three sheltering pines, Daniel's father came out onto the porch, limping slightly and leaning against one of the posts for support. He was in his late forties, and a good-looking fella when he smiled, Daniel had always thought. They had the same dark hair and sharply defined features.

"Where have you been?" he bellowed across the drive, as Daniel exited the truck. "Winston busted out of his stall. I need you to go look for him. Luke hasn't gotten back from town yet, and I can't find Austin anywhere." He turned away, evidently unaware that Daniel had brought home a guest. He was mumbling something about hating Sundays and not being able to get good help.

Daniel swore softly under his breath. Sunday was technically an off day for the ranch hands, not that anyone ever really had an off day on a cattle ranch. They had probably made themselves scarce on purpose, because inevitably, something would always turn up, and his father wasn't able to help out as much since the accident had left him with a bum leg.

His face was apologetic as he turned to Lucy. "Ever been on a horse?"

Lucy gave him a nod. "Is it possible to grow up in Silverton without having been on a horse?"

They both chuckled.

"I'd love to help," she said, clambering out of the truck and waiting for Shiloh to hop to the dirt beside her.

She slammed the passenger side door, and they began to walk in the direction of the barn.

As they approached, a cacophony of loud barks filled the air. Shiloh's ears shot up, and he took off towards the sound.

Lucy started to run after him, but Daniel placed a staying hand on her back. "He's fine. That's just Jackson. The only thing we need to worry about him doing is attempting to lick Shiloh to death. Shiloh good with other dogs?"

She nodded in response.

Sure enough, once they entered the barn, they found the pair checking each other out, tails wagging happily. Jackson, a Blue Heeler mutt with a Golden Retriever attitude and a blue patch over his eye, finished his examination of Shiloh and trotted over to greet Lucy.

"Needs a bath," Daniel warned, as Lucy stooped down to greet the animal.

"Wheew. Yes, sir-ee," she laughed. "And a Tic-Tac," she joked, as Jackson poked his nose directly into her face.

Daniel proceeded to saddle up two horses, while Lucy watched interestedly and handed him supplies from the tack room. When each strap was secured and he had let down the stirrups, he handed her the reins to a chestnut mare. "Her name is Chloe. She's very easygoing."

Lucy smiled, then placed a foot in the stirrup, grabbing the horn as she threw her other leg over. Daniel moved forward and adjusted the stirrups to her long legs, trying to keep his mind on the task at hand with her thigh nearly pressed to his ear. He could feel her warmth against his cheek without touching her. "What makes you think I need a docile horse?" she queried, a hint of snark in her tone.

"Wouldn't everyone rather ride a docile horse?" he sighed back, straightening.

Lucy did not deign to respond, but when she guided her horse from the barn, she gave him an impish little wink, and danced the mare in a circle.

"Show-off," he muttered grudgingly, mounting his own silvery stallion.

"So, do you have any idea where we might find this... Winston... was it?" Lucy glanced around, and his eyes followed hers. He saw her taking in the vast fields and treed hills with an expression that hinted at appreciation, swiftly followed by unease. "We might as well be looking for a needle in a haystack," she said.

Daniel indicated a distant grove of trees that sat low in a far-flung field. "Might have headed over that way. Little bit of cover from the wind?" A rough gust gnawed at the back of his neck as he spoke, and Daniel cast a glance at Lucy's outfit to make sure she'd be warm enough.

They headed in that direction, the dogs following. As the patch of pines and leafless oaks grew larger, Jackson lifted his head, sniffing at the air. He barked, and the two dogs sprinted out ahead, not stopping until they reached the wooded area.

Daniel dismounted beneath a tall spruce and tied his horse to an old, forgotten fence post sticking out of the ground nearby. Lucy did the same.

"Bugger is probably lounging about by the creek," he said casually. He pushed his hat up a bit. "Hear it?"

She nodded and followed where he led as Daniel stepped onto a well-traveled game trail. They'd only walked a few yards when a wild, excitable yipping met their ears. He pushed aside a low-hanging branch to see Shiloh and Jackson wagging happily at a young colt, who was dancing his feet, irritable with having been caught.

Daniel reached down to pat Jackson's head. "Good boy," he praised, but as he began to straighten, Shiloh tapped at his pant leg, causing him to let out a low chuckle. "You too, Shiloh. Good boy." He extended his other hand to dispense the required attention and then glanced at Lucy, smiling. "It's a good thing I have two hands."

"I'll say!" She shook her head at the pups, then glanced at the horse, now happily munching on a patch of grass. "That didn't take nearly as long as I thought it would."

Daniel shrugged his shoulders. "You grow up on a ranch all your life, you learn the popular spots." He went back to his saddle and returned with a lead rope. "Let's head back." He pointed to a patch of dark, furling clouds that were rapidly approaching. "We'll be lucky if we don't get caught in it on the way."

They made their way back to the barn at a quick trot, Winston, the colt, tailing resignedly after them, but they were still a good quarter mile from the barn when the first drops of rain began to *plop-plop-plop* atop their heads, and within moments, the sky had opened up and exuded a deluge that would have made Poseidon proud.

They cantered into the barn in a mess of wet animals and shrieking laughter.

Water droplets scattered down onto the dust-coated earth around them as the pair dismounted and settled the horses into their appointed stalls. The dogs shook roughly, splattering Lucy, and she wiped aggressively at her chin in response. "Thanks, boys," she said sarcastically.

"Nothing like taking a gal horseback riding and then dipping her into a bucket of freezing water just to impress her."

"Were you trying to impress me?" Lucy asked nonchalantly, as she squeezed the water from her dripping hair. Daniel glanced up, caught her eyes, and then found his gaze lingering over her body. He cleared his throat and redirected his attention to the tack room door.

The rain pelted against the tin roof of the barn, sounding like gunfire. It was coming down harder now. Outside the vast door, great drops were hitting the ground and bouncing joyfully into rapidly growing puddles.

"Should we wait it out?" he asked, scratching at the damp skin on the back of his neck. "It'll probably let up in a sec. You must be freezing... Hold on. I've got an extra coat I keep in the tack room."

He returned with an old blanket, his spare coat, and two water bottles from the flat they always kept beside the grain buckets.

"There's less of a breeze in the end stall there. The big one. We keep a bit of hay in there as well."

He spread the blanket over three bales and sat down with his back against four more, turning to see Lucy facing him in the doorway to the stall. He tipped his hat at her. "Saved you a seat."

Lucy appeared to hesitate for a moment before perching herself on the edge of the blanket right next to him, her hands on her knees. The air between them crackled a bit, but when her arm brushed his, Daniel realized that she was shivering.

"Coat. Coat. Here. Sorry. It's so freaking cold."

She stripped off her jacket with a chuckle and settled into the wooly one he held out for her.

"Sorry. Best I can do in the circumstances," he murmured. "Thirsty?"

"Mmmhhmm. Thanks."

Daniel was so busy trying not to watch her that he spilled his own water down his shirt front, which made Lucy laugh.

"At least you're already wet." She took another sip of water, then set it aside and leaned back on her elbows, listening to the rain. "I love the sound of rain on a tin roof," she whispered. "When I was a little girl, I would spend the night at my grandmother's. I used to love it when it would rain. I would open the window so I could smell it and snuggle into a real feather bed, and then I would fight to stay awake just to listen to the sound..."

At least when she was speaking, Daniel had an innocent reason to look at Lucy. She was such a unique combination of features—eye-catching and contrasting. Like the opposite colors on the color wheel. Her hair was hanging behind her head in damp, darkened strands, just brushed the top of the hay behind them. "I wish I had my camera," he said suddenly, interrupting her without meaning too.

"What on earth for?" she laughed, opening her eyes to cock her head to the side.

Daniel coughed into his hand. "I'm not trying to be weird or anything. It's just that... these are my favorite moments to capture. The simple ones that are just a little breathtaking."

Lucy turned on her elbow toward him, looking warmer, despite the lingering dampness of her clothes beneath his borrowed coat. She had, at least, stopped shivering, and this comforted him slightly, although he had no idea why. "You sure don't talk like a cowboy," she murmured, shaking her head. Then she corrected herself. "Well, sometimes you do. Like when you talk about the ranch. I can see you love it. But when you talk about your photography... you sound like a poet."

"Well. Butter my butt and call me a biscuit," he quipped, and she burst out laughing.

He leaned back, propping himself up on his elbow so that his posture mirrored hers, noticing as he did so, that his heartbeat was slowing, his racing thoughts calming. He was reveling in her ease. It was infectious. "Let me take your picture," he prodded, already guessing the response.

Lucy frowned and shook her head at once. "We're not that far from Portland. You could find any number of city girls there that would be happy to pose for a handsome fella like yourself. Just put out a model call on Facebook or something." She waved her hand dismissively.

"What if I don't want to photograph random girls from Facebook. Not least because it sounds kinda... creepy." He laughed. "What if I want to photograph you?"

Lucy ignored his question, changing the topic. "I think the rain has let up a bit. We'd better make a run for it." She hopped up and helped him fold the blanket. They stood by the barn door, looking out at the rain-drenched property for a second, then they took off running. Daniel led the way, the dogs—having leapt up from lazy lounging positions against the far wall—following hot on their heels.

He led them away from the main house and down a short gravel path to a collection of tiny cabins situated at the other side of a round paddock.

"Quarters for the help," he said with a wink, indicating the one he occupied.

On the porch, next to the door, was a snowflake-patterned umbrella. Lucy grinned at Daniel when she spotted it, and he shook his head. "Hindsight is twenty-twenty." He opened the door, inviting her in. "My experience with umbrellas is that they are never around when you need them."

Knowing Lucy would be coming today, he had tidied his space up a bit. The kitchen, which was tiny, occupied the left-hand corner across from the front door, and it was still shining from the scrubbing he'd given it this morning. His bedroom was through the door beside it. A small couch and a desk where his laptop sat filled the only other available space.

"Bathroom is through there if you need it," he pointed, but she wasn't paying attention.

"Be good, boys," he muttered to the dogs, before shutting the windowed door in their eager faces.

Still wrapped in his woolen coat—which made her look even smaller than she already was—Lucy meandered around the tiny room, gazing at the pictures on the walls. She touched the frame of a shot featuring an elderly man sitting on a tree stump, his dog by his side, a shotgun resting on the ground and pointing skyward in his other hand. His lined face evoked a sense of weariness and wisdom, trials and tribulations—at least for Daniel.

"Did you take all of these yourself?" she asked through an exhale. "They're..." Daniel held his breath. "Really... beautiful."

"You think?" He felt his shoulders relax.

"Yeah... I mean. I'm no professional. I don't know anything about the photography industry... but you could sell this stuff, couldn't you?"

"Some of it, maybe. I'd need model releases... and this one here..." Daniel nodded. "That man, Lou, was a ranch hand. When he became too infirm to ride, we let him stay on. This was the only life he'd ever known. We were his family. But he passed away last year—couldn't get a model release from him now. So, I shouldn't sell it." He chuckled. "That doesn't matter to me though. Most of these were taken just for me. You know?"

Lucy smiled. "I think that's my favorite. Look at his eyes... You must miss him."

"Yeah. We still have his dog, actually. She stays close to my father. He won't ever say it, but I think he enjoys having a shadow."

"What's her name?" Lucy asked, as she moved on to another photo.

"Her name is Morgan. Maybe you'll get to meet her when we schedule our shoot."

She didn't look up. "Persistent, aren't you? Do you ever give up?"

He shrugged. "Not when I find something I want." A light blush tinged her cheeks. The sight of it made him smile. He wondered idly what she thought of him. Did she still think he was handsome? It'd been a long time since high school.

Lucy turned and her eyes flickered over the rest of his domain. "So, you stay here instead of the main house?"

He sat down on the sofa. "It's better this way. I can have my own space, and Dad doesn't have to gripe about my pictures and tell me what a waste of time photography is."

"Just because he doesn't understand it now doesn't mean he won't understand it later on down the road," Lucy murmured. She passed him on the couch and reached down to squeeze his shoulder. Her touch was casual comfort at its finest, and Daniel hadn't felt casual comfort since he'd lost his mom.

"There's Jackson." She pointed to a photo of his dog lolloping through a field of high grass, smiling. "Who is this?"

"Mom," he answered. "She really liked my stuff. Or I think she did. Aren't all mothers supposed to love everything about their children?" He laughed. "She was biased."

"She was beautiful." Lucy looked out the window. A small shift in her demeanor and tone made him look around. "It's getting late. I probably need to get back home. I have a crazy day at work tomorrow. I'm sure you have a full day, too."

Daniel was surprised and—although he tried to hide it—disappointed. He wasn't ready for her to leave. He thought they'd have dinner.

"No problem. One sec."

He stepped into the bedroom to swap his shirt for a dry one... maybe leaving the door open on purpose... just so that she *might* notice his bare chest. He felt her eyes on him, but when he turned to the living room, tugging his shirt down, he found her innocently perusing his other photographs.

He grabbed a dry jacket for himself.

"It'd be cool if you wanted to borrow a shirt. Wouldn't fit you at all, but it'd at least be dry..."

"Actually, that would be awesome."

Daniel tugged a black band t-shirt from his dresser drawer and tossed it at her. She caught it and headed to the bathroom.

When she emerged, his thoughts jumped into erratic patterns that required instant redirection, and he occupied himself in the kitchen, emptying the dishwasher.

She looked *dang* good in his shirt. Why? He had no idea. There was something about the way it draped her slender frame, falling casually off one shoulder, that forced a furious, possessive reaction in him. He'd never experienced anything equal to it, and it really *wasn't* okay. They weren't even... even really dating? Right? Why should he suddenly want to heave her into his arms and declare that she was his in front of the entire universe? Was this a date? He hoped it was.

As they drove back to her house, Daniel thought back to how she had responded to his photos. Her approval had sent a rush of hopeful determination through him. She understood.

Finally. Someone understood. And it felt so good.

Lucy sat beside him on the wide seat of his truck, her thigh bumping against his every so often. Shiloh hadn't been quick enough to claim the middle, and Daniel was quite pleased about it. All the way back, he wondered if he should reach for her hand, but... he wasn't able to pluck up the courage.

His tires gave a little squawk of protest as the truck ground to a halt outside her house. She'd left a single light on in the back bedroom, and he wondered if it was to discourage thieves. His mother had always left the television on when they left the house. It was odd. The crime rate in Silverton, Oregon, was next to nothing.

As Lucy unhooked her seatbelt, Daniel pressed again. "I was serious. About taking your picture. Would you let me? You've seen my stuff now..."

Lucy nudged Shiloh out of the open truck door, then climbed out herself. "I'd really rather…"

"C'mon, Luce." He gave her his most charming, cowboy smile. "It'll be fun, and I'll even take you to dinner after." Then he raised his eyebrows suggestively. "I'll even get you some *crème brûlée*…"

"Ugh. Fine." She looked up at him with a smile. "Saturday the tenth, maybe? Afternoon?"

"Should be good for me!" He'd have to remember that this girl was a sucker for *crème brûlée*. She'd had it that first night they'd gone out to dinner… She was still chatting.

"I think I'm off. I'll have to check the schedule. Here, give me your phone. I don't know why we haven't done this yet." She plugged in her number, then called her own phone. "There. I'll let you know for sure when I've checked."

They said their goodbyes, and he watched as she walked up the stairs and went into the house. Once she was inside, and he'd seen the kitchen lights flicker on, he backed out of the driveway and headed back to the ranch. The tenth. He didn't think he could wait that long to see her again.

JOSEPHINE BLAKE

Chapter Three

·•· ♥ ·•· ♥ ·•· ♥ ·•· ♥ ·•· ♥ ·•·

LUCY PLACED HER KEY into the ignition early Wednesday morning, her breath freezing in the air as she shivered against the cold. She really needed to find a place to rent that had a garage. Scraping ice off the windshield when she was already late for work was *not* a task she enjoyed—and she always forgot to warm up the car.

Lucy pulled into a parking space by the gift shop and got out, locking the doors with the little button on her key fob. As she got out of the car, she glanced down at a now familiar text from Daniel.

Good morning, beautiful.

Her stomach did a flip-flop as she hit a quick response.

She could see Shannon, her boss, through the window, loading the cash register. Lucy glanced down at her watch. Only eight minutes late. That wasn't *too* awful. Right?

Shannon unlocked the door as Lucy approached and stopped her with a ten-dollar bill. "Coffee. I need coffee, pleeeease. I'm dying."

Lucy scurried down the street to Lola's, the local coffee shop and diner. Every time she entered the diner, she felt like she had fallen into a time warp and been spit out in the 60s. The black-and-white checked floors, the sparkling, red-leather bar stools... There was even a juke box in the corner.

She approached the counter, smiling at Janie, her best friend, who was scrubbing a stubborn ring from the coffee pot off the dappled countertop. "Shannon needs her coffee, like thirty minutes ago," she said, rolling her eyes.

Janie giggled. "It's a rough morning when she falls behind."

"Tell me about it. I get the fallout!"

Janie handed her a double espresso for Shannon and the standard French vanilla with cream for Lucy. She took a sip of the French vanilla. "You're a gem," she sighed.

Janie placed the money in the register and counted out the change. "What time do you get off tonight?"

Lucy tilted her head back and forth in indecision. "Probably seven unless Shannon needs me to stay late to put stock out. We're almost done with the Christmas decorations though. You better get a move on in here. You know

Mayor Greenwood wants the whole of Main Street to 'sparkle!'"

It was Janie's turn to roll her eyes. "You mean every tree, every light post, and every garbage bin all the way down to the traffic light, plus the massive gazebo that can be seen from literally every spot on Main... oh wait... is that not enough? You're probably right. Maybe I'll put some mistletoe over the door."

Lucy chuckled.

Then Janie said: "Want to meet me at Sullivan's for dinner and a drink after work?"

"No singing?"

"One day, I'm going to get you up there," Janie declared as she handed Lucy the change. "It's very liberating!"

"I think I'll take your word for it," Lucy shouted over her shoulder, as she headed toward the door. The bell above the door sang out before Lucy had turned back around and she slammed into the hard chest of someone on their way in. Someone who smelled faintly of lumber and cocoa... and campfires? She raised her eyes to meet the laughter in Daniel's.

"Well, good morning, Lucy Bennett," he said, grabbing her by the shoulders to steady her. Her coffee left a single little splatter on the floor by his cowboy boots but didn't manage to completely evacuate the cup.

"Err, hi!" she said a little too loudly. "Hi," she lowered her voice, which had suddenly gone a little breathy because the air seemed to have somehow become just a bit thin. "Sorry. Wasn't watching where I was going."

"Really?" The corners of his mouth twitched as he held the door open for her.

"Don't forget, Sullivan's at seven tonight!" Janie called after her, giving Lucy a searching sort of look that told her that her interaction with Daniel had not gone unnoticed by her friend. She nearly groaned. Without a doubt, she was going to receive the third degree this evening.

Lucy gave her a brief nod, her cheeks so warm she had the sudden urge to press them to the cool glass on the front window of the next shop over. What was the matter with her? What was she? A freshman nursing a crush on one of the hottest guys in the senior class? *Yes.* That's exactly what she was. The familiar butterflies danced around her stomach as she practically jogged back to the gift shop, feeling eyes on her back.

Shannon looked up as she entered the store, and then she frowned when she caught sight of Lucy's face. "What's the matter?"

Lucy placed Shannon's double espresso on the counter and waved her hand in completely vague dismissal. "I just... ran into someone a bit unexpectedly. That's all." *Literally.*

Shannon raised her eyebrows. She was a freckly-faced woman in her fifties, with a shock of red hair that was as bright as any of the Christmas ornaments in the shop. She was quite a bit taller than Lucy—which wasn't saying much, as Lucy was only five-foot-two—and comfortably filled out. She was consistently complaining about her extra ten pounds, but Lucy simply didn't see it. She thought her boss was a very nice-looking woman, indeed.

"I realize it's cold out there, but you look as though you allowed a four-year old to apply your blush this morning."

Lucy, never one to be able to hide her emotions, felt her face grow warmer still. She fanned at it with one hand, then gave herself away when she turned at the very faint sound of the diner bell across the way.

Shannon followed her gaze, a smile playing about her face as one of the patrons exited the diner and opened the driver's side door of his big old Chevy truck.

"Ah. Daniel Moore. He's a cutie, ain't he?"

Feigning nonchalance, Lucy retrieved her apron and a dust cloth from behind the counter. "Sure? If you're into that whole 'I'm a rugged cowboy' alpha-male sort of nonsense."

Shannon wasn't buying it. "Ding. Ding. Ding. We have a winner!" she shouted gleefully. "You look like that little Santa Claus beside the leg lamp!"

Lucy glanced at the offending Santa, who was bright red in the cheeks and sporting a 'Merry Christmas' sign across his belly, then she sighed.

"It is Daniel then." Shannon allowed herself a victorious grin before leaning conspiratorially over the counter. "So, spill."

"There's nothing to 'spill,'" she hedged.

"Lies."

Lucy couldn't shut her out. Shannon was like a second mom. Lucy told her about taking Daniel home that night and about their dinner the next evening. Then she chatted about going out to the ranch, the horseback ride, the rain.

"Girl, you got it bad," Shannon chuckled when she'd finished.

"He's been... a nice surprise. I gotta say, but..."

"But what?" Shannon turned and began dragging a storage box full of twinkle lights to the front of the shop. "He's interested, right?"

Lucy shrugged. "I think so? He keeps asking me out. And he..." she stopped speaking at once, clamping her mouth shut tight, but Shannon, sensing a juicy tidbit, went after her like a dog after peanut butter.

"What? Tell meeeeee."

"Sometimes, when he looks at me... I feel like... like he sees me, somehow. He has a way of making me feel beautiful, and... it's a rare change, is all. It's not like I look anything like my beauty-queen of a mother."

Shannon straightened, turned, and placed firm hands on her shoulders, spinning Lucy to face her. "You know better than that. I've always told you how pretty you are. Maybe you'll finally start believing me now that someone else is in your ear." Her eyes turned mischievous. "After all, he's a handsome cowboy. If I were fifteen years younger, I'd go for him myself!"

Lucy swatted at Shannon with her towel. "Back up," she chuckled. "Dibs."

She moved over to the counter and opened a box of merchandise, taking out the packing slip and retrieving a pen from the jar beneath the counter. It was time to change the subject before she blurted out every secret feeling and thought she'd ever had about Daniel Moore. "Who knew Christmas tree keychains would be an item this year?"

Shannon's lips pressed together in frustration, but she seemed to deem it wise to allow the subject to drop. However, Lucy had the distinct impression that her boss had not yet finished her interrogation. She would have to get a better game face!

·•·♥·•·♥·•·♥·•·♥·•·

Daniel walked into Sullivan's at around ten past seven, knowing he would have to perform some hard-core groveling to make up for his behavior last Friday. As he made his way to the bar, he spotted the owner, Mister Branden Sullivan himself, and gave the man an apologetic sort of wave. Daniel took a stool at the corner of the bar, scanning the crowd, and waited for barkeep to make his way to him. Branden leaned across the bar a few minutes later. "Not interested in serving any troublemakers tonight, Moore. You best head out."

Shame swept through his gut like a wintery gust of wind, freezing his insides.

He looked Branden dead in his dark eyes. "Look, man. I'm so sorry. Seriously, how many times have you ever seen me like that? I shouldn't have caused such a scene. You gotta admit though... Janice can really hit a bad high note..."

Branden's look was wary, but he cracked a smile at that. "That she can." He sighed and rubbed a hand through his black hair. "What'll you have?"

Daniel ordered a beer with profuse thanks and tried very hard not to watch the door. He still hadn't caught a glimpse of Lucy.

If it hadn't been for her, he might have waited a touch longer to show his face at Sullivan's. Branden was a good guy, but he was a devil to cross. After a few minutes sitting at the bar and tapping his foot to the beat echoing from the overhead speakers, Daniel had to admit he was a touch relieved he'd swallowed his pride. The worst was over now. He had a cold beer in his hand, and Branden was back to his usual cheerful self. Daniel considered himself forgiven.

Finally, catching sight of Lucy on the arm of the black-haired girl he knew from the diner, he smiled in satisfaction—patience rewarded. All rosy-cheeked from the cold, and laughing at something her friend had said, he watched the two women settle themselves at a table in the corner of the room. Emboldened by his early success, Daniel paid for his beer and sauntered over, grinning from ear to ear. He wanted to laugh when Lucy spotted him. Her eyes went as wide as saucers and her cheeks flooded scarlet once more. She always seemed to be turning pink when he was around.

"Is this seat taken?" he asked, as he pulled out the extra chair.

"Nope! You're welcome to join us!" Lucy's friend piped up quickly. He noticed her wince a fraction of a second later, and the table wobbled slightly. No doubt, her shin would be sporting a bruise the following day. He would bet good money that Lucy had a mean kick.

He placed his beer on the table as he sat down. "Daniel Moore," he said, extending his hand.

"Janie Doyle, and it seems that you *two*," she elbowed Lucy in the ribs, "already know each other?"

Lucy gave him a sideways look, ignoring the implication from her friend by twirling her straw around her glass. "I'm surprised Branden didn't toss you out on your ear again, after last week," she said to him, taking a sip.

Daniel chuckled. "It was definitely on his mind. But... Branden has known me a long while."

Janie's eyes darted from Lucy to Daniel and back again. "Am I missing something?"

There was a brief pause between the three of them, during which someone hollered at the television over the bar. Then Lucy said, "Daniel had a rough night here about a week ago. I just helped him out. That's all. It was no big deal." She continued to twirl her straw; her eyes downcast. Ashamed to have been caught associating with him? Daniel certainly hoped not.

"If it was 'no big deal,'" said her friend, making air quotes with her fingers, "why are you blushing?"

Lucy glowered at her friend. "You're *not* helping, *BFF*." She layered sarcasm on the acronym.

Janie didn't look too upset about it. She just leaned back in her chair, watching them like a scientist about to carry out an experiment.

Daniel, shifting a bit uncomfortably in his seat, decided to throw himself into the line of fire. "I had too much to drink, and she took pity on me. She let me have her couch for the evening, and I woke up to a big sloppy kiss... from Shiloh."

Lucy shut her eyes as Janie's face broke into an expression of undefinable glee. "You didn't tell me you had a sleepover!"

The couple at the next table looked around curiously.

Lucy shook her head, now glaring daggers at Janie. "Daniel was the only one getting any sleep. I was tossing and turning all night because I had a *stranger* in the house!" The look she cast Daniel next might have made him burst into flames right then and there.

Daniel chuckled—his collar a bit hot—and took a sip of his beer before glancing at Janie. She winked at him knowingly, and he smiled. He would have to start tipping her better in the diner and make sure to stay in her good graces. It never hurt to have friends in the right places...

Janie started to take a sip of her drink, but they called out her name from the stage and she leapt up from her seat, leaving Daniel and Lucy sitting alone in a semi-awkward silence.

He leaned over to Lucy. "So, we're still shooting this Saturday, right? Did you check your hours?"

The look in her eyes became uncertain and shy. "I really don't know why you're so insistent..."

Daniel tipped his chair, grinning. "I'll pick you up at two on Saturday. You don't have to get in front of the camera... but I would love it if you would."

She toyed with the edge of her napkin. "Maybe check with me closer to the weekend?"

"I'll check back with you Friday night... maybe when I pick you up after work and take you to dinner again? What time do you get off?"

Her responding smile, in contrast to her dark expression when they'd chatted about her posing for him, lit up like the setting sun. "I have the early shift. Five? Make it six, so I can run home and change. You wanna pick me up there?"

"Friday at six. Sounds good." He stood up and tipped his hat to her. "Dress warmly."

She gave him a questioning look, but he just winked and set off for the door, leaving her sitting there with wheels turning behind her green eyes.

·•·♥·♥·•·

That Friday after work, Lucy dashed home in a nervous flutter to freshen up before Daniel picked her up. She let Shiloh outside for a minute and then went into a mad rush, trying to make herself irresistible in under fifteen minutes.

Shiloh's head was cocked curiously as he watched his mistress from a comfortable pile of pillows on the bed. His eyes followed her back and forth, his mouth hanging open; Lucy was utterly convinced that he was laughing at her.

Finally, she pulled on a thick green sweater that matched her eyes, jeans, and a pair of boots. She laid out a scarf, coat, and red hat, then swapped the hat for a white one, and nodded at the outfit in approval. She figured that if Daniel had said to dress warmly, he couldn't be planning to take her anywhere particularly upscale.

Her head shot up as a knock sounded at the door and Shiloh leapt excitedly from the bed.

Lucy paused before the long mirror in the hallway, trying to make sure she had managed to obtain a reasonable presentation of a human being. After a few more seconds of fussing, she darted to the door and pulled it open, hoping against hope that she appeared relaxed... as opposed to the frazzled mess she truly was.

Dang! He looked handsome. All cowboy charm in a red-and-black checked coat made of thick wool over a black shirt and dark jeans. His customary wide-brimmed hat was perched jauntily on his head, and his pointed boots shone as though they'd just been polished all over again. His grin was lopsided and cocky, and Lucy thought she spotted a glimmer of mischief in his blue eyes. She stepped aside to allow Daniel to slide past her into the living room, blinking a bit rapidly. "Give me just a sec," she said, smiling. "I just need to grab my things."

He sat on the sofa, seeming completely at his ease, and Shiloh promptly trotting up to his knees, demanding to be petted.

Lucy grabbed her coat and gloves. "So, where are we headed that requires me to 'dress warmly'?" she asked suspiciously.

He grinned. "I'll tell you once we're on our way, and you can't bail out."

She gave him a serious look. "I haven't heard any rumors about you being a serial killer or anything, but that sounds kinda sketchy."

He patted Shiloh on the head before he stood up and nudged Lucy out the door. "If you turn up missing, I'm sure Janie will make sure that I am on the top of the suspect list."

She had to laugh at that. Yes. Janie knew about her plans this evening. She had even offered to come over and help Lucy get ready. Janie was an eternal romantic. She just always seemed to choose the wrong sort of guys. The girl had had her heart broken so many times that Lucy could no longer keep count.

Glancing at Daniel and his easy stride, a vague sense of foreboding crept over her. She really wasn't good with heartbreak... But Daniel was a good guy, right? She's made inconspicuous inquiries here and there about town, and no one had a bad word to say about him.

"More backbone than most of the young fellas in this town," cheerful Missus Doreline had said, as she purchased a little Victorian house with sparkly snow atop its roof.

"That one? Real gentleman," Hannah Affrey had said with a wink, as she placed two 'baby's first Christmas' ornaments on the counter for her twins.

Janie smiled at Daniel now, framed as he was by the glittering Christmas lights that now illuminated her entire neighborhood every night. He'd been straight with her from the beginning. She couldn't imagine him doing anything to hurt her. *They all seem like good guys in the beginning,* whispered a negative little nay-sayer in the back of her mind. But Lucy ignored it.

Once inside Daniel's truck, she turned to him. "I'm in. Now, tell me."

He started the truck and pulled out onto the main road, grinning, and taking no chances. When he had driven two streets over and jumped onto Highway 213, he said, at last, "We're going ice skating."

Lucy's eyes widened in terror, and her cheeks heated again. Why did she always have to blush like an idiot when Daniel was around. "Really? Ice skating? I have a hard enough time putting one foot in front of the other on *not-slippery* ground. The last time I went ice skating was for a friend's birthday party, and I took out four other skaters when I fell!"

He snort-laughed. "I know. I was there."

Lucy covered her face with her gloved hands. "You were, weren't you? I remember being mortified and wondering if you had seen it."

Daniel squeezed her hand. "I told my friends to quit teasing you when they wouldn't shut up," he said. "It wasn't that bad..."

Lucy laughed ruefully. "I doubt the other skaters I took out would agree with you. One girl sprained her ankle, and another guy split his lip."

He shrugged his shoulders. "Sounds like the normal casualties of being a teenager to me. I doubt anyone made it to adulthood without a scar or two."

"True." Lucy grinned to herself. She had forgotten that Daniel had been there. Maybe she had pushed it out of her memory. His buddies had been pointing to her, laughing. She'd been so embarrassed, but she'd had no idea he had been the one to silence them.

He turned his head to look at her. "Have you been ice skating since?"

Lucy shook her head. "That was my first and last time."

"Let's give it another chance." He raised her fingers to his lips and gave them a gentle kiss that sent a shiver through her entire body. She tried to ignore her reaction... and the thoughts that accompanied it. Like... wondering what it might feel like if he pressed his lips to her neck instead....

She cocked her head to the side as she picked up a large black case that lay between them, attempting to distract herself. "What is this?"

"It's my camera," he replied as he turned onto the main highway. "I thought I'd bring it, on the off chance something neat came up."

Lucy grimaced. "You mean like me falling?"

"Something like that," he joked, and he turned up the radio to her protests, laughing at the expression on her face.

Three minutes later, they had arrived at large, decorative, wooden archway that marked the entrance to the Oregon Gardens. The botanical gardens just outside of Silverton put on a popular Christmas light display every year that included a skating rink, a Christmas market of crafts and goodies, and visits to Santa Claus for the children. Lucy had been several times, but never to skate.

Daniel bought a couple of sausage dogs and sodas and brought them to the table. "Not exactly the Silver Grille, but it will do in a pinch."

Her stomach grumbled in hunger as she accepted one of the hot dogs gratefully. "You certainly know the way to a woman's heart."

Daniel took a bite, then tore open a packet of mustard and squeezed it over his cardboard tray. "I thought that only worked with men."

"Okay. How about *my* heart?" Lucy chuckled as she sipped at her soda, already finished with her dinner.

He raised his eyebrows. "Might need to go get two more!"

She tossed a napkin at him playfully. "We still need to get our skates."

"What size do you wear?"

She told him, and he was off, hot dog in hand, weaving through the crowd.

Once they'd laced up, Daniel guided Lucy onto the ice, both of her hands in his. He handed his camera to a skater nearby. "Can you take our picture? I already have it set. All you have to do is focus and push the button."

Lucy looked at Daniel like he had lost his ever-loving mind, then glanced back over her shoulder when she heard the click of the camera. She turned her face in shock. It clicked again. If anything, the bystander was enjoying capturing her candid moments. Lucy glowered at Daniel, then at the innocent bystander.

Daniel, sensing impending doom, led Lucy to the wall, took the camera from him and patted him on the back. "Thanks, man."

"No problem."

Daniel grinned as he watched him skate away. "Smart man. You looked like you were going to take a swing at him."

"It'll be you if you don't get back over here, Daniel Moore."

At that moment, Lucy lost her footing. As he skated to her aid, she grabbed his hand. Two seconds later, they were on their backs. The stranger skated up and took a picture with his own phone. "You want this one, buddy, call me!" The man shouted as he skated off, his cackle echoing in Lucy's head.

Daniel was the first to get to his feet. He reached his hand out to Lucy.

Lucy wrapped her fingers around his and attempted to stand shakily. Then her foot slipped once more and knocked into Daniel's. There was a shout, a tumble, and then he landed flat on his back once more. He turned his head to look at her, wincing. "Good gravy. You're a danger to us all!" he guffawed.

Lucy managed to get herself into a standing position, using the wall for support once more. "I trusted you, Daniel Moore. Look where it got me." The smirk on her face let him know he wasn't completely in the doghouse. Give it another twenty minutes. If he kept it up, he would *certainly* find himself there, and *not* in Shiloh's doghouse. Much worse. Shiloh's doghouse had heat, food, and a warm bed. He wasn't getting any of that. Cold doghouse. And positively no goodnight kiss...

※ ❖ ❖ ❖ ❖ ❖

After they had meandered through the light displays, grabbed some fudge from a vendor, and picked a Christmas ornament from another stand, they headed for the parking lot, huddled together for warmth. Daniel took a risk then and slid his coat around Lucy, tucking her body close to his. When she didn't pull away, a soft warm glow blossomed in his chest.

Finally, safely ensconced in the truck once more, Daniel turned to look at her, a coy sort of smile playing about his lips. Her hair was messy, her cheeks were red with cold, and she was smiling. She looked beautiful. "How are you feeling?"

At once, her countenance shifted to a mock scowl. "I'm miserable, thank you very much.

There is going to be a bruise the size of Pluto on my hip."

She pointed a finger in his face when he started to laugh. "*Not* funny!" She settled back against the seat, her arms crossed over her chest. "Last time I ever let you pick the date."

"So, you admit it was a date, then?"

Lucy gave him a flustered look. "That's not what I meant!"

Daniel leaned back in his own seat with satisfaction and started the truck.

She popped him on the knee with her hand, and his grin widened.

"Get that smug look off your face!" she exclaimed.

The rogue within him decided to push her just a little bit further, and he said, as he accelerated back onto the highway. "So, if it wasn't a date, Luce, what was it?"

Lucy paused for a moment, her face twisting into a grimace. He could tell she was attempting to come up with some sort of snarky response, but before she could form a reply, a massive, lifted black truck shot out of a side road in front of them, causing Daniel to swerve swiftly to avoid a collision. His arm snapped in front of Lucy, protecting her body from the jolt as he braked forcefully to keep them from trundling into the ditch.

Daniel cursed loudly, shaking his fist at the windshield as the truck roared away, its taillights blazing insolently. "He could have killed us!"

They sat there for a few minutes, neither speaking. Daniel could hear his heart pounding in his ears. Finally, he looked at Lucy. "Are you okay?"

She ran a shaky hand through her hair. "I'm fine. We're good. All's good."

Daniel took a few minutes to collect himself and then pulled back onto the road.

He had this insane feeling welling up in him, brought on by the thought of what *might* have happened. What if he hadn't been able to stop in time? What if there had been a collision, or he had rammed into the ditch? What if something had happened to Lucy? What if he had lost her... like he had lost his mother. In a flash. In a single act of carelessness... What if. What if. What if.

They drove the rest of the way home in silence. When they pulled into her driveway, he walked her to the door, patted Shiloh on the head, and left with a promise to pick her up on Sunday.

As he drove home with nothing but the grumble of his truck for company, Daniel tried to sort out what he was feeling. It wasn't as though Lucy was the first girl he'd ever dated; he'd had a lot of dates with a lot of different girls.

But... he couldn't ever remember feeling like this before. He wondered idly if love was worth the inevitable loss that came with living. Love? He shook away the thought. He wasn't in love with Lucy Bennett.

Chapter Four

· ♥ · ♥ · ♥ · ♥ · ♥ ·

Lucy examined herself critically in the full-length mirror in her hall. She had taken extra time styling her hair. It fell in gleaming curls about her face. Her jeans hugged her body, while the fitted red sweater and brown suede jacket she had chosen added a sophisticated flair. But... still...

Shiloh's bark sounded from the backyard before the slow, insistent knock at her door. A nervous smile was playing about her lips as Lucy opened it, tucking a bit of hair behind her ear.

There he stood, leaning against the railing of the porch, and looking at Lucy as though he'd quite like to eat her up. "You look *good*, Miss Bennett." The inflection in his voice made a shiver jump down her spine.

She stood there for a moment, a little dazzled, and then a little awkward.

"Ready?"

Coming back to herself, Lucy shut the door behind her, and then sighed and closed her eyes in annoyance, her hand still on the door handle. "One sec. Forgot my hat."

Daniel gave her another admiring look as she got into his truck two minutes later. "Yep. Always gotta have a hat." He flicked his own for emphasis and winked.

He took the highway out of town. Lucy stared absentmindedly at the passing countryside. "Today's the day you finally kidnap me for good, isn't it?"

Daniel chuckled and turned off the main road. "Naw, figured we'd just shoot out at the ranch, maybe do a few black-and-whites, for drama, and several full color shots. Personally, I think black-and-white will tell your story better, add an air of mystery."

She toyed with a strand of hair as she pondered that. "I don't think there is anything mysterious about me at all."

Daniel turned to look at her, smiling coyly. "Beg to differ."

They pulled up in front of the main house, Jackson springing off the front porch to greet them, and Lucy lamented the fact that she hadn't asked to bring Shiloh along. A few moments later, a small border collie made her bumbling way over to them.

Daniel crouched down as she approached, and the collie nuzzled eagerly into his hands.

Looking up at Lucy, he said, "This is Morgan. You recognize her from that shot of Lou?"

Lucy took a seat on the cold gravel, patting the spot beside her for Morgan to join her. The elderly dog sidled up to her and lay down by her side with a satisfied huff, and Lucy ran her fingers through the collie's fur. "You've seen some things, haven't you, old girl?" she asked the dog quietly. "Oh, the stories you could tell. Do you know all of Daniel's secrets?"

The sound of quiet clicking made her head snap up. She hadn't noticed Daniel slink off to his truck and return with camera in hand.

"Didn't realize this was part of the shoot..." she mumbled, tensing immediately.

"Naw. Relax. The camera knows when you get nervous. It's like a horse." He winked. "It's just me and you here. Go on, pet Morgan some more."

Beyond self-conscious, Lucy pushed to her feet, dusting the dirt and grass from her jeans, and ignoring Daniel's look of disappointment. "So, what did you have in mind?"

He rallied at once. "I was thinking we could take a couple of the horses into the corral. I know you're comfortable with them, so I'd love to just let you work with them a bit. You can take Winston through some paces. He likes the corral." He grabbed her hand, leading her in the direction of the barn. "I have a few ideas!"

The next hour or so was spent with Daniel focused on getting the perfect shot and Lucy trying to pretend that there was no camera anywhere near her. They moved from the corral to the barn, to the field, to the trees, and after a little while, Lucy found this sort of easy flow within herself that she hadn't anticipated. She would turn to Daniel, look over her shoulder, lift her hair into the wind, spin on the spot. The camera became nonexistent. She would look past it, to Daniel, and listen to his directions.

"Lift your left hand high, great, now step forward, turn your right hip to me a few inches. Perfect. Now drop your hand. Look over your shoulder. Spin. Awesome. Can you sit there? Cross your ankles. Look at me? Look to the left. Chin up a little more."

Somewhere in the middle of the shoot, Lucy realized she was having the time of her life. She laughed easily. Spun. Danced. Posed. And it felt strangely natural to her. This was easy. This was...fun! She hadn't expected that at all.

An hour later, they were standing beside a fence that ran along the outskirts of the property. Across the frosty field, they could see the farmhouse, barns, and little cabins, all looking like iced gingerbread houses. The sky, threatening snow, had gone purple with the setting sun, and flashes of gold were making yesterday's light snowfall sparkle.

"Come on," said Daniel, and he slung his camera around his back to keep it out of the way. "I'll help you. Sit on the edge of the fence with your right side facing me..."

Without warning, he scooped Lucy's feet out from under her. She laughed as she caught herself on his neck, and then... they both stilled.

The abrupt closeness, the sudden warmth of their bodies colliding, their breath misting before them on the cold air, it was all causing a rush of sensation that made Lucy's brain go numb.

Jackson barked.

Daniel cleared his throat. "Ah. Yeah. So. Here..." He set her down on the top fence post. "Brace your hands here." And he lifted her hands. All Lucy could think was that his were so warm. They were calloused from farm labor, and he was so solid. She didn't know why she was surprised, but Daniel's body was taut and lean, and he smelled like fresh air and heat and pines... She was leaning into him... her side curled against his chest, and it felt so perfect...

"There. That should. Yeah." Daniel moved back, letting go of Lucy and she slipped. He caught her. They both laughed.

"We might need to finish up," he said, glancing skyward. "Looks like it could snow again."

Lucy clambered back up onto the top of the fence as Daniel's prediction came true and the first, glistening snowflakes began dropping onto their heads.

"Ah. No! Not again!"

"What's wrong?" Lucy said.

"It's just...first rain. Now snow. It's ridiculous! And..."

"Can't you shoot in the snow?"

"Yes, but dinner..."

Lucy grinned and threw back her head, laughing. She'd never felt so free, never so beautiful. "Then, let it snow, cowboy."

They finally paused once the sun finished sinking down behind the foothills and dusk truly settled in.

"Annnnd, the light's gone," Daniel smiled. "Dinner?"

"Yes, please. I'm starving."

As they made their way back across the field, Daniel was flicking through his camera, gazing intently at the tiny, digital screen. "I think..." he said as they walked. "They're all amazing, but this shot... with the snow. This might be the best one of the day!"

"Don't show me," Lucy said, suddenly wary.

Daniel raised an eyebrow at her, but shook his head, smiling.

"Really, they're all great. Thank you so much for doing this."

"It was fun! I didn't think it'd be so much fun."

The day had been overcast, which Daniel said was the best lighting to work with. "I thought you'd want a sunny day," she commented, as they circled the barn and approached his cabin.

"Naw, you tend to end up with a lot of over-exposed shots when there's too much light. I was a bit worried about the light reflecting off the snow, but..." He stepped inside his cabin, flicked on the lights, and unloaded his gear onto the couch. Then he rubbed his hands together, warming them up. "Hold on. Don't take your coat off. Did you know we're supposed to have a meteor shower tonight?"

Lucy nodded, plopping herself down on one of the little chairs surrounding the kitchen table. "I heard something about it on the news a couple of days ago. I didn't realize it was happening tonight."

Daniel smile. "Yep! You game?"

Her skin seemed to tremble at the very thought of stepping back outside. "It's awfully cold, and what about dinner...?" Her stomach rumbled loudly to emphasize her words.

He gave her that mischievous grin she was beginning to associate with tumbling into his arms. "I think I have that covered. Trust me."

Lucy cast him a dubious look as she hauled herself back to her feet.

"After you," he said, collecting two stocking caps from a rack beside the door and passing her one. Lucy frowned but did as she was bid.

As Daniel casually took her hand and led her down a worn path, she noticed him still grinning lopsidedly. He had something up his sleeve... whatever it was had better involve her getting *warm*!

The path twisted past his cabin, through a copse, and to a small clearing that opened bit by bit to reveal an inlaid fire pit, two chairs, a cooler, and a large stack of thick blankets. The dusting of snow from earlier decorated the entire clearing.

Lucy grinned as Daniel produced a lighter from his jacket pocket, released her hand, and crouched down near the obviously pre-laid fire pit. Within moments, the kindling had caught, and orange flames began licking their way over the wood. An orange glow fell over them, casting deep shadows in the surrounding trees.

The light caught the self-satisfied, male cockiness shining from Daniel's eyes as he withdrew a thick blanket from nowhere and wrapped it around Lucy's shoulders. She smiled her thanks, and he indicated one of the chairs. She sank into it, gratefully, her feet aching. Then she shivered, gripped the arms of the chair, and dragged it over the dirt so that she could be as close as possible to the fire without actually climbing inside the ring of rocks.

At the sound of a cork popping, Lucy looked around and grinned. "You've been a busy guy."

"Why, whatever do you mean by that, Miss Bennett?" Daniel decanted two glasses of red wine and passed one to her, then withdrew a pack of sausages from a butcher shop in the next town over.

Lucy's stomach growled again in response to the beer brats, and Daniel laughed. "I thought they might be a step up from plain old hot dogs. Here," he handed her a roasting stick. "I've got plates and ketchup and mustard in the cooler, too."

A few minutes later, they had both gone silent as they chewed. Lucy, for her part, was thoughtful. Her mind had locked onto a self-sabotaging sort of anxiety as she thought about Daniel flicking through all the ridiculous pictures he had taken of her that afternoon. She could not help the words that popped out of her mouth next. "This is... really wonderful. But you've gone through so much trouble. Why are you doing all of this? I mean, it's just me." She ended on a shrug.

Daniel took a seat beside her, propping his roasting stick against the wood pile. "Why do you always say things like that?" He smiled at her defensive expression and placed a reassuring hand on hers. "I just mean... you seem to have this idea that... that no one should..." he frowned, and Lucy could tell he was struggling for words. "You just seem like you think you don't deserve to be... cherished."

He flushed at his last word and his eyes skated away from hers.

Lucy played with the edges of the blanket. "I don't know. I guess I've just always felt that I... fall short, somehow."

"By whose standards?"

Well, my mother's, for one. But she didn't say this. There was no use harping on about how she'd grown up with a fit, fabulous beauty queen for a mother, and how she'd never felt like she could measure up.

"I think once you see the pictures from today, you'll see what I see. You're beautiful, inside and out. There's a kindness in you that makes its way out in your eyes—your expression. You're... different, in this amazing way, Lucy, and I... I so desperately want you to see it."

Their eyes caught. Lucy's breath stilled. For a moment, she could see herself in his eyes. And for that moment... she felt beautiful again. *He* made her feel beautiful.

Jackson came ambling over, rolling on his back and groaning beside Lucy's chair. She took the cue and reached down to rub his belly, laughing. "He's very subtle."

Daniel shook his head, chuckling. "There is *nothing* subtle about Jackson."

"How long did it take you to pull all of this together?"

Daniel threw a few more logs on the fire. "I got up early."

A chilly wind whipped through the trees around them. But snuggled in her blanket, with the orange heat of the flames dancing over her cheeks, Lucy hardly felt it.

"I wish I would have had a heads-up—I could have at least chipped in and brought stuff for s'mores or something." She grinned at Daniel and elbowed him as he sat down.

"Nah," he said, chuckling and bending over the arm of his chair. From the pouch dangling there, he withdrew graham crackers, marshmallows, and peanut butter cups, then he winked. "I like surprises. Anyways... gotcha covered, sweet tooth. I also..." He seized two paper cups and showed her his thermos. "... brought hot chocolate."

Lucy squealed with delight, and Daniel laughed so hard that a snoring Jackson jerked, then sat up and cast them a bleary look of disapproval.

Exhaling, with a broad smile on his handsome face, Daniel's eyes shifted to the sky. "Hey, I think I just saw one!"

Lucy straightened up, following his gaze. "You know? I forgot all about the meteor shower."

Daniel took her hand and tugged Lucy to her feet. He reeled her to him, and Lucy felt absolutely no desire to resist when he pressed her to his chest. "I forget a lot of things when I'm with you," he whispered.

Lucy gazed up into his eyes, and she could see the firelight reflected in them.

Slowly, Daniel lowered his lips to hers.

The heat that built between them was slow, and impossibly perfect. When Daniel's mouth first pressed to her own, Lucy was still smiling, but within a few breathless seconds, the blanket had dropped from her shoulders and onto the dirt, unnoticed by either of them. Daniel's hands slipped down to Lucy's hips, and he tugged her body against his own, using the loops of her jeans. The stars overhead began to gleam and flash against the velvety blackness of the night as Lucy inhaled the scent of heat, smoke, and pine, and clean, cold Oregon air.

It was perfect. If she could have stood there, wrapped up in his warm embrace forever, Lucy thought she just might have done. When they finally parted, the frigid air slipped between them, and Lucy nearly tugged Daniel back to her. He placed his forehead against hers, and then tucked her into his chest, neither saying a word.

They roasted marshmallows.

♥•♥•♥•♥•♥

Three days later, Lucy was opening the store. When she unlocked the door for customers, Daniel was there to meet her. He handed her a cup of coffee, grinning in that self-satisfied way of his that made her think he was up to something.

She smelled the contents. It was her usual French vanilla with cream. She glanced at him curiously. "How did you know?"

He grinned. "I may have had a little bit of help from Janie."

She rolled her eyes. "So, you've been manipulating my best friend into giving away my secrets? I'll have to have a talk with her."

Daniel raised his hands in innocence. "All she did was tell me what kind of coffee you like."

Lucy's eyes narrowed. "Now, it's just coffee. But what's next? It's a slippery slope." She chuckled and took a sip. "Thank you."

"What are you doing for lunch?" he asked.

She shrugged her shoulders. "I packed one. Why? Wanna share?"

Daniel patted a leather binder he was holding. "I have something I'd like to show you." His fingers drummed excitedly on the front cover.

Lucy swallowed roughly as her eyes caught on that leatherbound case. She knew what it was at once... and she didn't want to see it. She hadn't been photographed since her last school pictures. How long had she spent dodging cameras? Only to have her *boyfriend*—she still got a bit of a thrill from that word—end up being a dratted, albeit talented, photographer!

She shook her head. "I'll meet you for lunch, but I really... I don't think I want to see them, Daniel."

His shoulders fell, and he cocked his head to the side in a very characteristic gesture. "You... you don't even want to see them?"

Lucy lowered her eyes from his. "When I'm with you, I feel beautiful. Seeing the pictures will... bring me back to reality. I am well aware of my limitations."

Daniel took a step forward and took her hand in his. Before she was aware of what he was doing, he had pressed his lips to the back of her knuckles. A jolt shot through her entire body. "What limitations?" he whispered against the skin there.

Her tongue seemed to have swollen to twice its normal size. "I—"

"You," he said, bringing his head down so they were on eye level, "are only limited by that little voice inside your head. Let me tell you a secret." He brushed a strand of hair from her cheek. "That little voice is lying."

"Daniel..."

The bell above the door gave a chime as the front door opened, and Lucy sprang away from him as though her skirt had suddenly caught fire.

"Mom! Hi!" She cried, too loudly. Then she coughed, blushing to the roots of her hair. "What... er... what are you doing here?"

Spinning about, Daniel whispered. "Lunch is at twelve-thirty, right?"

Lucy nodded numbly and made a shooing motion with her hand as her mother paused to examine the display of snow globes. She straightened as Daniel passed her—tipping his hat—and turned to watch him go. Her expression had gone from curious to suspicious in a half a second flat.

"Was that Daniel Moore?"

Lucy nodded, and hoping to distract her mother said, "What brings you into town?"

"Do I have to have a reason to visit my daughter? I haven't seen you in ages, and I have some shopping to do. I thought maybe we could have lunch. There's a new little place over..."

"Oh, Mom! You should have called. I... uh... already have plans for lunch." Lucy hoped that would be the end of it.

No such luck! Her mother gave her a probing look, and Lucy could tell she was making the very connection Lucy had hoped to avoid. Her eyes narrowed. "What kind of plans?"

The candy display next to the counter suddenly became very interesting. "I'm just meeting a friend. It's no big deal." Her finger tapped at a marshmallow pop in the shape of Frosty the Snowman.

"Would this friend happen to be Mister Daniel Moore?"

Lucy felt the blood rush to her cheeks. There was no mistaking her mother's tone. "What if it is?"

"Should you really be encouraging him?"

A streak of hot anger bubbled to life in Lucy's chest. She spun on the spot, no longer embarrassed, but beyond irritated. *Why?* Why did her mother always have to be like this! "I believe I can make that decision for myself."

Her mother's mouth flattened into a thin line of disapproval, but she evidently wished to avoid an argument, because she said, "I just don't want to see you get hurt, dear. Keep your eyes open. That's all I'm saying. So. How's about lunch on Sunday instead? You could come over after church."

·•·♥·♥·♥·♥·

Daniel was at Lola's by noon. Janie spotted him in an instant. He watched her refill coffee cups all around, then she slid into the seat opposite his at a booth in a far-flung corner. "So, how did it go?"

Daniel picked up a packet of sugar, flipping it through his fingers, and trying to form his thoughts into words. "She doesn't want to even see the pictures..."

"Well, I knew that would happen."

"I just don't get it. She's a pretty gal! I've never seen someone with such horrible self-confidence issues."

Janie patted his hand. "I'm glad *you* see it. I think living in her mother's shadow has been difficult for her." She nodded at the picture hanging just behind his head, and Daniel turned around to look. Sure enough, there was Missus Bennett. She was a good deal younger than the woman he had just tipped his hat to in the gift shop, and she was very pretty indeed, standing on a float in the middle of the Silverton 4th of July parade, waving at the crowd.

"She's spent her whole life having people tell her that she's the spitting image of her father. No one much liked her father, not even her mom, so... you can imagine..."

Daniel nodded his head slowly, and then glanced up as Janie waved through the window.

"She's here. That's a good sign." Janie scooted out of the booth. "Just give it time. You're the first guy she's been interested in in years. Make her look at those shots you got of her. They're amazing. I'd better get back to work before Lola sees me slacking off." Janie greeted Lucy as she approached the table.

"Dishing out more dirt?" Lucy joked, but Daniel saw her give her friend a searching look.

"All of it. All the dirt!" Janie laughed, and she danced off to clear a table.

Lucy removed her coat and slid into the seat across from Daniel. "You and Janie sure seem to have become besties all of a sudden. Don't believe everything she tells you," she told him.

"Careful. I know the good stuff." Janie shouted from two tables over. "Like that time you left your keys in the freezer and I had to give you a lift to work for two days before you found them. Or that time—"

"Thank you, Janie!" Lucy cut her off, laughing. "Aren't you supposed to be... I dunno, working?"

Janie didn't seem too scared. She returned, took their orders, and went back to the kitchen, chuckling to herself.

Lucy was still shaking her head at her friend when Daniel popped his leather-bound portfolio onto the table between them.

He didn't give her the chance to protest before withdrawing the top photograph. Sliding her cutlery out of the way, he set it down in front of Lucy who blinked down at it in confusion. "Daniel, I—"

"Just look."

It was a colorful shot of her kneeling on the ground, stroking Morgan. It was his favorite, mainly because she had not known he was going to take the picture. The photo captured her warmth and sincerity as she affectionately stroked Morgan's fur. It had been taken at a side angle. Her hair fell in riotous curls about her face and her eyes were blazing with happiness. Everything about the image was perfect. The sunlight was at her back, shining through her hair. It had only taken a few adjustments in Lightroom to make the image pop. The beauty was all Lucy.

She needs to see herself the way I see her, he thought.

And he held his breath.

For a moment, Lucy just sat there, staring down at the image. Then she smiled. It was a soft, disbelieving sort of smile. "That's me?" Her eyes rose to his. "How did you do it? Photoshop?"

Daniel shook his head. "I didn't do anything to it. I adjusted the white balance. Upped the saturation a little and brought the blacks down a bit to... sorry. Nerding out a little. Point being, the images didn't need any major adjustments. That's who you are. That's who everyone sees but you."

Lucy flipped to the next picture... and then the next. "You made me look..."

"I didn't *make* you look beautiful, Luce. You just are, all on your own." He took her hand. "You're very inspiring. Can we shoot again sometime?"

Janie gave an exaggerated cough as she approached "'Scuse, lovebirds, but I have your plates."

Lucy's face turned pink. Daniel loved it when she blushed.

There. He'd done it. She'd seen them now. Dare he pose his next question? He closed the binder, moving it to the side of the table to make room for their plates.

"So… you took direction extremely well when we took these. And your movements are so fluid. You held poses perfectly and found several of your own. I think… I think we should submit these shots to one of the modeling agencies I have connections with in Portland."

Lucy nearly spat out a bite of mashed potato. Her eyes were watering, as she began to laugh. "You're joking."

"I'm not."

Daniel watched her register the seriousness in his eyes, and the sparkle that she always seemed to carry around with her seemed to die, leaving behind an under-exposed representation of Lucy.

She placed her fork down firmly. "No."

"Why not?" he asked in frustration. "You've seen the pictures. I didn't alter them, and you were great in front of the camera. You needed a few minutes to warm up but then…"

But Lucy shook her head, determined. "The talent is all you. You're an incredible photographer. And sure, every girl *dreams* about becoming a model one day, but I don't think there's any sort of real future in it for me! They'd never take me. I'm too short, I'm not… I'm not anything to look at, Daniel. No modeling agency would ever sign me and I'm not really into the idea of being officially told I'm not pretty enough," she laughed again, but it was colder this time, and Daniel could sense her walls flying back up.

He opened his mouth to try and persuade her further, but the look in her eyes made him swallow his argument.

They finished their meal in silence, both a little tense. Afterward, Daniel walked her back to the gift shop. "Listen," he said, grabbing her hand as she made to stride inside. "I pay an arm and a leg to work with models that move as naturally as you did in front of the camera. I've paid a few hundred dollars to work with people that weren't half as good as you were the other day. IF an agency wanted you to work with them, would you?"

She paused, took a breath and then said, "Of course I would. I think..." she sighed, rubbing her eyes. "I think it would be an incredible experience. I had so much fun with you during your shoot. But Daniel, I'm just being realistic."

The wheels in his head were turning when Daniel climbed into his truck a few minutes later. He had asked, and she had said... He sighed, and then lifted Lucy's portfolio and examined the images within. She was good. Too good. And what was more... she had loved being in front of the camera. He hadn't imagined she would be quite as talented as she had been, most people weren't.

Thumping his knuckles against his knee, Daniel sighed again and cast a glance towards the door of the Pansy House Gift Shop. Lucy was going to be angry with what he was about to do, but he was going to have to risk it. If she wasn't going to fight for herself, he would.

·•·♥·•·♥·•·♥·•·

Lucy watched Daniel move off in the direction of his truck through the front window display and shook her head. *Modeling?* The idea had never really even crossed her mind. It wasn't feasible for someone who looked like her to aspire to be a model. In fact, it was downright laughable.

Shannon thanked her for closing up that evening as she left through the back door of the shop twenty minutes later. "By the way, the displays all look wonderful. Really. And I love the snow globes! Nice touch!"

Lucy smiled and waved her boss out of the gift shop. She was heading back to the counter when she registered what Shannon had actually said. "She's a nut," Lucy chuckled, shaking her head. "I didn't do the snow globe display, she did."

Her eyes darted over to the display in question, and she wandered absently over to it, dust cloth in hand.

There at the front was the petite little gal with curly hair, falling into the arms of a cowboy, both of them in ice skates. She smiled at them.

They reminded of her disastrous ice-skating date with Daniel, then she gazed passed them to the five other snow globes... and... *well, it must be a series,* Lucy thought. The same couple was featured in the rest of the snow globes as well. Lucy cocked her head to the side.

In the one to the right, just behind the ice skaters, the couple was surrounded by animals. Dogs and horses, and they were laughing. The one on the left... *what in the heck?* Lucy lifted the snow globe out of its nest of fluffy, fake snow and examined it critically. The cowboy in this one... he had a camera slung about his neck, and he was dancing with the curly-haired gal... who was wearing a red sweater...

Don't be ridiculous, Lucy thought to herself. *It's just a coincidence.* But as she replaced this one and examined the fourth snow globe on the display, she could not help the shiver of foreboding that crept down her spine. In this one, the couple were standing on opposite sides of a fence, their arms crossed and their backs to one another.

Lucy set the snow globe back on its fluffy cushion without looking at the final one in the series and went to count the register. *Don't be stupid,* she told herself again. *Snow globes cannot predict the future.*

·▾·▾·♥·▾·▾·

That weekend, Daniel and Lucy joined Janie at Sullivan's for open-mic night. Janie signed up for a few songs and came back to the table. "Thanks for meeting me tonight." She grinned at them both. "I hate to be a third wheel, though."

Lucy was watching Daniel chatting with the bartender, but she looked around at Janie's words and shook her head. "You're not a third wheel!"

Janie's expression was highly amused. "Soooo, Daniel showed me the photos he took. They were incredible! Have you heard anything back yet?"

A moment of confusion passed between the two friends. Then something cold slid into Lucy's chest. She looked out the window, watching the Christmas lights twinkling in the darkened gift shop across the way for a moment. Then she murmured, "What are you talking about?"

"The modeling agency in Portland?" Janie's look of enthusiasm turned to puzzlement. "He... said he sent them off earlier this week."

"Did he now?" It wasn't really a question.

"Oh."

Janie straightened and her eyes found Daniel across the room.

Lucy's mind had gone blank.

"He didn't tell you."

"No, he did not. In fact," Lucy stood up and glared at Daniel as he returned to the table. "I vividly remember asking him *not* to."

Daniel, his hands full of drinks, took a moment to register the situation unfolding before him. He was sliding glasses onto the table, grinning. "Janie, take that will you, before I drop..." His smile slid off his face like maple syrup off a hot waffle.

"What did you say, Luce?"

"I said," Lucy growled, climbing to her feet and wrenching her coat off the back of her chair. "That I vividly remember asking you *not* to send the shots you took of me to that agency in Portland. Or..." She paused, a finger to her cheek in mock thought. "Or did I imagine that conversation?" She shoved her arms into the sleeves of her coat, ignoring the whining screech of the karaoke singer that had just begun a horrible rendition of *Silent Night*, and staring directly at Daniel. He cowered as her fury broke over him.

"Luce, look... you said you would give it a try if they wanted you to come in, okay? I was only going to tell you if they called you in!"

"Isn't that... illegal or something?! You can't do that! Don't you need some sort of release to do something like that??"

Daniel blanched.

"I just want to prove to you that you *could* do it if you wanted to. I..." He gazed around at Janie for support, but Janie was looking stony-faced.

"I didn't know you hadn't told her."

Lucy's arms were crossed so tightly in front of her chest that the buttons on her coat were pressing harsh lines into her wrists.

"Lucy, I was only trying to help. I would never try and hurt you. I just... you even *said* that you *would* do it if they wanted you!" he repeated, now sounding a bit desperate.

"No agency is ever going to want to work with me!!" Lucy heard herself shouting. "You can't... you can't just mess with people's lives like that, Daniel! How *could* you?"

Daniel began stuttering a response about trying to boost her confidence, but Lucy suddenly found that she had no desire to hear it. She held up a hand. "I need to go."

"Luce," Janie reached out a placating hand. "C'mon. We can talk about this."

But with a last furious look at Daniel, Lucy spun away. She saw him rising from his chair, clearly intent on coming after her and she whirled around sharply.

"*Don't* follow me. I need a minute."

Holding her head up high, she stalked out of Sullivan's, feeling his eyes on her the entire way. The silence on the street outside was deafening. As Lucy flew off down the sidewalk, flakes of fresh snow began drifting down onto her heated cheeks. She dashed them away with the tears.

JOSEPHINE BLAKE

Chapter Five

•·❤·•·❤·•·❤·❤·•

Lucy's alarm went off early on Sunday morning, thankfully pulling her from the dream she'd been having. In it, she had been standing inside the window display at the Pansy House Gift Shop, showing off the latest merchandise. Townsfolk she knew kept passing by the window, and when they saw her there, they pointed and laughed. Her mother had been there. So had Janie and Daniel, and they had been laughing right alongside everyone else.

Lucy hugged Shiloh's neck, burying her face in his fur. He gave her hand a little snuffle, then panted enthusiastically. On the bedside table, her phone went off. Groaning, Lucy stretched across the bed and retrieved it. A picture of Daniel snuggled up next to her cheek at the Oregon Gardens popped up. She let it go to voicemail.

She sat by her mother at church, who kept asking her what was wrong, and after the service, the two solidified their lunchtime plans.

"I put a roast in the crockpot this morning! It seemed like the thing for a day like today." Her mother lowered her long, thick eyelashes as she affected a little shiver.

It was, indeed, very cold. Their breath was rising in a mist before them in the church parking lot. The sky overhead was full of clouds that threatened snow again at any minute.

"I'm just going to run home and grab the little cupcakes I made this morning. Anyone else coming?"

"Nah." Her mother tossed an arm around her shoulders. "It'll just be us. I feel like I've hardly seen you lately."

Lucy was inwardly thankful for her all-wheel-drive sedan when she pulled onto the slushy, gravel driveway that led up to her mom's little cottage across town. It was a single-story affair, with a small front porch, but it was decorated so lavishly with garlands and mistletoe and lights that you would have thought Savannah Bennett was anticipating the mayor.

She knocked on the front door, then let herself in and inhaled the delicious smell of cooking pot roast. "Mom?" she called out.

"In the kitchen!"

Lucy made her way towards the sound of her mother's voice, passing not one, not two, but three massive Christmas trees, all fully decorated. Lucy shook her head.

"You're going to have to come and help me do mine," she said, indicating the tree as her mother wiped her hands on a red-and-white checked kitchen towel.

"I know! If I don't do it, who will?"

Lucy let out a laugh. She spent so much time decorating at the gift shop that her own house was often neglected during the holiday season.

"Hey, I've still got two more weeks," she said defensively, popping her cupcakes onto the counter.

Her mother raised an eyebrow at her.

"Oh stop, Mom. They're Keto-friendly."

Looking much happier, Savannah Bennett turned, lifted the lid of her crockpot, and poked at the roast.

"I think it's done. Hungry?"

Lucy nodded. She hadn't had much of an appetite as of late, but something about her mother's home cooking always made her stomach growl. "It smells amazing."

Her mother waited until they were both seated at the kitchen table with their meal before starting on her.

"What's going on?"

"Nothing! I'm fine," Lucy told her, shrugging her shoulders.

"Lucy Bennett, you most certainly are *not* fine, and if you want any pot roast at all, you will tell your mother what's bothering you." She speared a carrot on the end of her fork and pointed it accusingly at Lucy from across the table.

"Withholding pot roast? Is that allowed?"

"Pretty sure it's in the '*How to Interrogate Your Daughter*' handbook."

Lucy stood and grabbed two glasses from one of the cabinets, filling them with ice and water, as she tried to decide what to reveal.

At last, sitting back down, she swallowed and sighed.

"Remember Daniel Moore?"

A wary expression slid over her mother's face. Her chin rose into the air a bit, like a hound scenting a rabbit. "Of course."

"Well. Okay. You might have been right."

Instead of looking smug at these words, like Lucy had expected, she was surprised when her mother's expression softened. "Tell me."

And it all came spilling out of Lucy's mouth.

"He's a really good guy. Really, he is. I just... I just can't believe he would go behind my back like that. It's not like I didn't have fun. And I was a little taken aback by how nice the pictures turned out, but..."

"You've never mentioned modeling before, Lucy. Why would he think you were interested in it at all?"

"I guess..." she hesitated. "I guess because... I don't know. Mom... He keeps telling me that he pays hundreds of dollars to work with people that don't have half the natural talent I had at our little shoot. But Mom... I don't get it. I'm so... plain. I'm not pretty. I'm nothing like you! Everyone always tells me I look like Dad." Lucy felt her eyes well up. "And Dad..."

"Well, honey, your dad might not have been the best husband or father, but I'll tell you what..." She sighed. "He was *a looker*. Plain? No. Don't you ever call yourself plain. That's the most ridiculous thing I've ever heard you say." She reached across the table and tilted Lucy's chin up so she could look directly into her eyes. "You are beautiful. Just because you resemble your father doesn't mean you are anything like him at all on the inside. You have such a good heart..." She drifted off, smiling fondly, and Lucy saw her eyes sparkling. "Good gracious.

If you think you are ugly in any way, shape, or form, I have *failed* you as a mother. You are the prettiest girl in this freaking town." She let go of Lucy's hand to dab at her eyes.

"But..."

"No."

"I—"

Her mother held up her hand. "Lucy, did you have fun modeling for... this photographer fella?"

Lucy quieted. "Yes."

"And you were comfortable and happy doing so?"

"Yes."

"Then why in the heck wouldn't you want to try to give it a go professionally if someone with *experience* tells you that you have a talent for it? Heck! You could be on the next ad for my favorite bubbly water!"

Lucy giggled and took a comical drink from her water glass, tossing her hair around until it flopped in her face. "Oh yes! Drink Sunshine Spritz, it'll make your day bright!"

Now they were both laughing. Lucy shrugged and took a bite of her lunch. "It really... it might be fun. But... there's nothing like being told you're not pretty enough by a bunch of strangers..."

"Lucy Anne! I don't want to hear that you think you're not pretty enough ever again for the rest of my life... and yours! I will haunt you," she threatened jokingly. "It sounds like he asked if you would be interested before he did it."

"Yes, but I told him..."

"And you'd never have done it on your own."

"No, of course I wouldn't—"

But her mother was smiling. "Maybe I should get to know this Daniel a little better. Why don't you bring him around for dinner in a week or so… after you've patched things up."

"Mom."

"Lucy Anne, I know my daughter. And I know you've been wanting something more. Take a chance, girl. See where it leads you."

"Who are you, and what have you done with my mother?" Lucy questioned. "Weren't you just warning me against seeing him the other day?"

"I suppose that's a fair point to make," she replied. "But that was before he came to talk to me the other day."

Lucy nearly choked on her pot roast.

"I respect any man that can sit down with a girl's parent and ask for permission to date her."

"But… but what did you *say*??"

"I said I'd like to talk to Lucy first."

· ♥ · ♥ · ♥ · ♥ · ♥ ·

Daniel sat on the front steps of his cabin, rubbing Jackson's ears and gazing out into the yard. A couple of chickens pecked at the hard ground, casting him dubious looks. Daniel had tried to call Lucy every day for the last week, but she had never picked up, and never returned any of his calls. He sighed.

She was obviously still furious with him. He'd blown it. The first girl he'd ever loved, and he blew it. *Loved*. There was that word again, floating around in his brain. He couldn't love Lucy Bennett. She was perfect, yes. He adored her in every way, yes. But... he'd only known her a few short weeks! And... he'd lost her trust. "You idiot," he reprimanded himself. "She asked you not to do it, and you did it anyways. Of course, she's furious with you."

Daniel stood up and dusted his jeans. The day was over. The work was done. Maybe a hot shower would perk him up. He was about to turn and head inside when his father appeared around the corner.

"Hey, Dad," he said, forcing a smile onto his face.

Daniel's father was sour faced with pain as he limped to his son's side. "This came special delivery for you. I thought it might be important."

Daniel looked down to see a thick, yellow envelope. He took it, thanked his father, and sat back down on the porch step, patting the seat beside him.

Rodger Moore hitched up his jeans and settled himself down beside his son, breathing heavily.

"How's your leg?"

"It'll be better when the cold is gone." Staring off into the distance, he said, "We haven't really talked much since we argued, and I wanted to say I'm sorry... but you've seemed... distracted. What's on your mind? Anything I can help with?" He gave Daniel a rueful grin.

Daniel looked at his father, puzzled. "What brought this on?"

His father laughed. "Do you think I've lived all this time and can't recognize love-struck when I see it? Is it that girl you brought over a few weeks ago?"

Chagrined, Daniel nodded. "I think I messed it up, though, Dad. She won't answer any of my calls." He stared at his hands dejectedly. "You know, it was all fine before. I didn't know what having her in my life could mean, so I didn't know to miss it. Does that make sense?"

His father placed a comforting hand on his shoulder. "More than you know."

They were silent for a few moments, then his father murmured. "You love her?"

"No." Daniel responded, so quickly that his father smiled.

"You know," he said, stretching out his hand to Jackson, "I was the same way when I fell in love with your mother. Fell quick and hard but didn't want to think it. Didn't want to say it... But that love... it was a risk worth taking, let me tell you."

"Was it though?" The pain leached into Daniel's voice. "Was it worth it? We lost her."

Rodger clapped Daniel softly on the back of the head.

"Wouldn't change it for the world. I'd have her back, of course, if I had the choice. But I would never give back the time we had. Never trade it. Not for anything. Would you?"

"Never," Daniel sighed. "Sorry. That was a dumb thing to say."

"Love hurts... and it's a risk, giving a little bit of yourself to someone. But you know... someone once told me..." He grinned and quoted:

"'Because someone we love is in Heaven, there's a bit of Heaven in our home.'"

Daniel smiled. "You got that off that Christmas card from Aunt Sal, didn't you?"

"No less true!"

The pair laughed.

"I think you'll figure it out, Son," Rodger said as he stood up, leaning on his cane. "Sometimes, a grand gesture is in order."

"Grand gesture?" Daniel asked, frowning up at his father in the dying light.

His father rolled his eyes. "Have you *never* seen a romantic comedy?"

Daniel shook his head. "Not my thing."

"Your mother used to make me watch the Hallmark Channel all the time." He waved his hand. "Go... chase the girl through an airport or something..."

Chuckling, Daniel watched his father hobble two steps and then he said, "Hey, Dad?"

"Hmm?"

"I'm sorry, too."

"I know, Son."

Daniel listened to the screen door on the main house let out its usual squawk as it opened and shut, then sat there for a few more seconds before he remembered the envelope his father had brought with him. He slit it open and withdrew its contents, reading intently. Then he grinned. There. This was it.

He knew *exactly* what to do!

·♥·♥·♥·♥·♥·

It was a Thursday night, and Lucy was closing up the gift shop early on Shannon's orders.

It had snowed non-stop for the last two hours, and they were calling for a good four inches of accumulation. Christmas music was playing softly over the speakers.

Just hear those sleigh bells jingling, ring-ting-tingling, too...

"C'mon, it's lovely weather for a sleigh ride together with you..."

Lucy jumped.

Daniel was standing by the front entrance, smiling awkwardly. She hadn't heard him come in.

"You haven't returned my calls."

Lucy plodded over to the register and began shifting through the day's receipts. "I... I was actually planning to call tonight."

"Were you?" Daniel's face brightened. He approached the counter slowly.

"Look, I..." he stopped and shifted from foot to foot.

Then Lucy turned, and they both spoke at the same time.

"I'm sorry."

Daniel raised an eyebrow at her. "You're..."

"Sorry. Yes. I... I overreacted. I..." She swiped a sudden tear away from her cheek. "I'm not super happy that you submitted those pictures, and I was..."

"Completely right to be furious with me. I never should have done it. Not without telling you. I just... I saw how happy you were, and how *good* you were... It doesn't excuse it. But..."

"You meant well."

Daniel nodded.

"All right."

"All right?"

"Yes, all right."

Daniel raised an eyebrow at her and lifted an envelope she hadn't realized he was carrying. Lucy's eyes danced to it and back up to his handsome face.

"They'd like you to come in for an interview session."

Frosty, the snowman, was a jolly, happy soul! With a corn cob pipe and a button nose and two eyes... Michael Bublé got through four more lines before Lucy could stutter a response.

"They want... me?"

"Yes. And..." Daniel stepped forward and placed the envelope on the counter next to her. "If it makes any difference... so do I."

Lucy flung her arms around him.

Something was going on at Lola's diner down the way.

Lucy and Daniel exited the gift shop giggling, flicking off the lights and locking the door behind them. "What do you figure they're up to over there? It's going to storm. They should be closed," she said, pointing around the hood of his truck.

"Let's go see." Daniel took her hand, and they headed in the direction of the little diner.

"It's freezing out!"

"C'mon, it'll just be a minute, maybe Janie will give us a cinnamon roll to take back to your place and we can watch a movie and have cocoa."

Lucy snorted. "She won't just give us *one* of those massive cinnamon rolls, she'll give us *three*, and we'll be in a sugar coma for a week. You're nuts!"

Daniel grinned at her. "Possibly. Nuts about you, at least."

He guided her over to the diner, passing lines of lit trees on Main Street, and pulled open the door.

A roar of warmth and sound greeted them, and Lucy nearly stumbled backward with the shock of it. The entire diner had erupted into applause. People were whistling, cheering, and Janie was standing on a swivel barstool, hollering at the top of her lungs:

"CONGRATULATIONS!"

All around the room, hanging from thin string banners, were the photographs Daniel had taken of her. Black-and-white and color, smiling, frowning, surprised, sitting, standing, dancing. Lucy's own face was looking back at her from every corner of the room. She turned to stare at him.

"It was just... one more surprise."

He winked.

Lucy kissed him again.

Lucy's mother trotted over the moment they broke apart.

"This is great, hon. Really. These are beautiful." Happy tears filled her eyes as she embraced Lucy and turned to Daniel. "Fine." She said, grinning, "You may date her... and thank you... for showing her the beauty inside herself."

Daniel tipped his hat, his cheeks a bit red.

There was a minor distraction at that moment that involved Janie jumping up and down on the barstool, and promptly falling as the seat swiveled beneath her feet. She shrieked and landed in the arms of a tall young man wearing a thick vest over a red-checked flannel.

"Janie?!" Lucy shouted over the crowd.

"I'm good! I'm good!" Janie was laughing, embarrassed as she apologized over and over again to the man that had caught her.

Daniel started over, looking concerned, but Lucy grabbed his arm. "I think... she's well taken care of."

She raised her eyebrow and indicated the fella that had caught Janie. Then she said, "Thank you for this."

He handed her a drink. "Anything for my gal."

Janie appeared, took hold of Lucy's arm, and pulled her aside. "Isn't it exciting?" She looked in Daniel's direction. "You are going to forgive him, right? He put this whole thing together, had me call all of your friends. There are a lot of people in this town who love you, Lucy... and I'm pretty sure Daniel is at the top of that list."

Lucy glanced over at Daniel, who was now conversing quietly with a man who looked very like him. "I think he might be at the top of mine, too."

•˙•˙•˙•˙•˙•

Daniel looked up, catching Lucy and Janie eyeing him and giggling.

He took a breath and turned back to his father.

"This is... a pretty incredible talent you have, Son. It would be a shame for you to waste it."

Daniel's eyebrows raised questioningly.

The senior Mister Moore chuckled. "I know I haven't been extremely supportive of this. But..." He looked around at Lucy, then at all the pictures of her hanging about the ceiling. "If this is really what you want to do, I want you to do it. I want you to do something that makes you happy. I like farm work. It feels good. It's my life... but until recently," he knocked his cane against his bad leg. "It never occurred to me what it might feel like to have something you love to do... and not be able to do it."

"Dad, I know how much the farm means to you. It means a lot to me, too," Daniel told him. "I don't think it has to be one or the other. Maybe we could hire an extra ranch hand, free me up a little bit, so I can see where this goes?"

His dad smiled. "Okay. Let's do it."

"Daniel!!!"

Daniel swung his head around to see Lucy standing next to a collage he'd done of their ice-skating outing. She had her hands on her hips and a stern look on her face that he would have been worried about if her lips hadn't been twitching.

He walked over to stand beside her. Everyone clustered around them, laughing. At the center of the collage was the picture of the two of them lying flat on their backs after falling. It wasn't a great shot. It was a little blurry, and Lucy's hair was standing on end. Daniel's hat was covering half of his face.

"How did you get that one?" She laughed, pointing. "It's horrible!"

His eyes were full of mischief. "You really didn't think I would let that picture escape?" He chuckled. "I got his number. He was only too happy to send it to me."

Lucy punched his arm playfully.

Daniel turned her to face him. "What is that saying? *All's fair in love and war*?"

Lucy glared at him. "Is this love or war?"

He lowered his face to hers. "Maybe a bit of both?"

The whole room began cheering all over again. They hardly noticed.

Later that night, after the crowd had fled in the face of the oncoming snowstorm, Lucy followed Daniel to his truck. It was parallel parked in front of the gift shop.

"Forgiven?" he was chuckling.

Lucy kissed him again. "Fine. You're forgiven."

All is calm. All is bright.

"Wait, is that music?"

Lucy looked around. "Drat. I must have forgot to unplug the iPod. I better run in real quick."

"Still up for a movie?"

"Sounds good."

Daniel held up his box of cinnamon rolls. "I'll go turn on your car to defrost your windows, then I'll follow you over."

Lucy nodded and let herself inside the gift shop. It was dark, but the place always managed to be cheerful. She made her way through the displays, smiling, her mind happy, and paused when she spotted the snow globes nestled into their fluffy cotton nests. A streak of light from a streetlamp outside illuminated their little figurines inside. They had been... rearranged. Shannon must have done it. But when? Little white specks were swirling around and around inside the glass orb at the front. Was there a fan?

Lucy came right up to the display and picked up the one whose snow was spinning in lazy circles. She turned it over, looking for a switch, but found nothing but an ordinary knob, and it wasn't spinning. She flipped the snow globe over, peering at it, and then smiled when she saw the little statue within. The little petite gal with the long curly hair and the handsome man in a cowboy hat were locked in a close embrace.

The woman's foot was kicked up, and they were laughing.

Shaking her head, Lucy replaced the snow globe on its shelf and went to turn off the music. She joined Daniel by her car and gave him one last kiss before climbing into the driver's seat.

Glancing curiously through the gift shop window as she pulled away, Lucy was sure she saw the little snow globe display twinkling merrily at her as she drove past.

・❤・❤・❤・❤・❤・

The End

・❤・❤・❤・❤・❤・

About the Author

•·♥·•·♥·•·♥·•

JOSEPHINE BLAKE IS A *USA Today* Bestselling Author and an Award-Winning Graphic Designer. She enjoys a quiet life on a comfortable piece of property in her very own small-town in the Willamette Valley.

With over 20 published books in the romance genre, Josephine works hard to make sure her stories bring a little more love into this crazy world.

She and her husband spend most days chasing their little one around their farmhouse with thankful hearts.

Notable Works:

Josephine Blake's debut Historical Romance novel, *Dianna*, hit the shelves in August of 2016 and became a bestseller two years later. Her Gothic Historical Romance novel, *A Brush with Death*, followed suit later that year in 2018. Yours at Yuletide became her very first Contemporary Romance release in the winter of 2019.

Sign Up for her newsletter to stay up to date on every new release at www.awordfromjosephineblake.com.

Also by Josephine Blake

•·•·♥·•·♥·•·♥·•·•

The Brittler Sisters Series
Dianna
Little Rose
Charlotte
Sarah-Jane
Noelle
The Heart of Hope

•·•·♥·•·♥·•·♥·•·•

The Brides of Adoration

JOSEPHINE BLAKE

Maid in the West
Cowboy, Take Me Away
The Arms of a Stranger
Nursing His Heart
Sweet Love of Mine
Brenden's Bookish Bride

·❤·❤·❤·❤·❤·

Love in Unity Springs
Yours at Yuletide
Second-Chance Santa
Mistletoe Miracles
Candy-Cane Kisses
Christmas in Unity Springs-Series Collection

·❤·❤·❤·❤·❤·

Standalones
Two Hearts, One Stone

·❤·❤·❤·❤·❤·

Multi-Author Projects
The ABC Mail Order Brides-Emeline's Exile
Charming Tales-Little Red
Silverpines Series-Wanted: Lawyer and Wanted: St. Nick

Josephine Blake also Writes Gothic Victorian Romance under her middle name, Elizabeth.

Titles by Elizabeth Blake

The Hands of Fate Series
A Brush with Death
A Twist of Fortune
A String of Lies

Standalones
Dark was the Night

JOSEPHINE BLAKE

Printed in the USA
CPSIA information can be obtained
at www.ICGtesting.com
JSHW030307250924
70368JS00010B/35